Cried Out The River For Love

Charlotte Fairbairn

Dear Shudoa
with love from
Charlotte x .

Published by Linen Press, London 2022
Maltings Lodge
Corney Reach Way
London
W4 2TT
www.linen-press.com

A CIP catalogue record for this book is available from the
British Library.

Cover photograph: © arcangel-images.com
Cover design: Lynn Michell
Typeset in Sabon; printed and bound by

ISBN 9781919624822

About the Author

Charlotte Fairbairn was born and brought up in Scotland. She read languages at Somerville College Oxford, then lived briefly in London before moving to Cumbria where she has spent all her adult life. Her first novel *A Bear with an Egg in Her Paws* was published in 1999 by Citron Press. In 2002, she won a two-book deal with Headline under the Review imprint and *God Breathes his Dreams through Nathaniel Cadwallader* was followed two years later by *With the Sound of the Sea*.

Charlotte is Head of Content at Lowther Castle near Penrith and is a co-founder of Spiracle Audiobooks.

She has two (grown-up) musical children, a dog called Bear and a houseboat in Rotherhithe.

Praise for Charlotte Fairbairn's writing

'A fable in the Paulo Coelho mould.'
The Bookseller

'A simple and beautifully imaginative story of a mythical land.'
Glasgow Evening Times

'Mythical and supernatural elements are blended with a sense of foreboding...'
Waterstones Review

'A poetic allegory with hints of Thomas Hardy and a dash of magic realism, the book is about the divine nature of art, and is set in an entirely imaginative countryside, described in vivid beauty and harshness.'
Harpers and Queen

'An imaginative tale of a world which time forgot, loss of innocence and the devastation of betrayal.'
Buzz Magazine

'Richly imagined. Fairbairn ...is hailed as a coming name on the literary scene.'
The Scotsman

To my mother

Elizabeth Fairbairn
(1938-2021)

who loved spoons

&

To our friend

Will Lowther

forever

INTRODUCTION

STOP THE CLOCK

On the day when they heard, mother and father, that their daughter was found, on the day when it all came to an end and they could stop looking, they could stop waiting, her husband was on the old barge by the old deal wharf, in the city, on the river going east. Isabella was backstage in the theatre, in the costume room, it was all brocades and buckles and bits of feather and glimpses of flesh. Someone burst in – Isabella had pins in her mouth and she was on her knees with a thigh before her and a woman above that and a hem here, some bias binding – and the voice said she has been found, Sybilla, your daughter, she is found. Isabella spat out the pins. She dropped the hem and the binding and she climbed through her boots, onto her legs and ran past the woman from the room and all she could say inside herself as she scrambled through stage curtains, over stage-edge, down steps, up steps, through balcony, through lobby, out into blinking light, was she is found, she is found, she is found.

As she rushed towards him, along the street, along

the river, in and out of the wharf buildings, towards the old barge, Isabella pictured how it would be when she shared it with Eustace, this news. She saw herself holding the words with him, puffing them out through the bands of his hair, blowing them out through the grip of him, through the cling of him. She needed to feel the news for herself, understand it, learn it, know it and she clicked along the river, she ran, she stumbled, her crimson red platform heel boots crinkling more with every step because she was moving fast and they were not used to that. The sun shone and it was hot, direct-hot like a fixed stare. The moon-and-stars clock ticked to the tock of the day unseen and in her mind, while she hurried along, while her boots clacked, while the back of her neck burned, she heard the tick and the tock, back and forth. Isabella came closer to the barge and the noise of her breath grew louder, beating in time to the clack of the boots and the tick tock back and forth of the out-of-sight moon-and-stars clock. She could see her husband's outline, his bowed back jutting up over the parapet of the deck. He was bending over, making something. She could not see what he was making but she could hear it, the hee-hee-haw of the jig-saw and the occasional grind of the feet of the saw-horse as it shifted under his efforts along the deck, under his frenzy which was like steel, only harder.

'Eustace! Eustace!'

Above the noise of the saw and the frish of the water and the flap flap of the mast ropes around the basin, he did not hear her.

'Eustace!'

She was half way along the jetty, nearly at the barge and she was overflowing, unravelling, a bit of sweat, a bit of slipping of her coat and her hair and those wretched bloody boots and why didn't he hear her, why didn't he look up.

'Eustace.'

She had reached the steps and now she climbed them, boots almost off her feet, stumbling over the deck towards his still bowed body, now her coat down off her shoulders and her arms outstretched but at an angle.

There was a tree along the wharf side and today in the sun, it cast shadows over the measured, held-back, undoing, breathless, bursting-heart journey Isabella was making towards Eustace. The tree was an oak, full-boughed and it had watched the river go by for as long as the city had reached this far. The tree saw the woman walk along the gangplank of her story, treading upon the shadows of its branches. The tree felt the woman's heartbeat thumping like the tide of the river upon its roots. The tree saw the bent-over man at the end of the woman's sight. The tree did not hear what was said, what was shouted, did not know if it was joy or grief, but it saw the man rise up, his back straighten, his face alter, a shank of hair fall over his eye while his gaze locked with the woman's. The tree watched while the man remained glued to the spot and the woman moved inexorably and clumsily forwards.

Stop the clock. That is what the tree would have said if it had known, if it could speak, if it could feel, if it had all the facts, all the story. As the woman reached the man, as their hands touched, as her face swept his into its embrace. Stop the clock. The tree would have reached out to the clock with the stars on its face that sat unseen in the wheelhouse gazing inwards away from the deck and the tree would have placed its finger gently onto the smiling lips of the moon.

Sshh, the tree would have whispered, sshh.

Stop the clock.

WAS THERE A BEGINNING?

Was there a beginning?

Were there many beginnings?

Was there something that led to her being lost in the first place?

Or many things?

Could you count them?

Was it like the river and no one could tell you where it began or where it ended, where the first drop was or the last? Could the pair of them, the father, the mother intertwine their hands and stand together and make notches on the face of the clock of their lives and retrace the path of each one, each drop, after she was found, after it was over. And look back? Could they? Could she? And what about the father who adored her to the heavens and back? Could he?

THERE WERE THREE SETTINGS

There were three settings.

The beaten up coal-barge by the deal wharf on the river in the big city going east.

The hills, the cliffs and furthest reaches of her imagination, the sky that cloaked their farm, their farm.

The river.

THERE WERE FOUR CHARACTERS

There were four characters.

The father, the mammoth, the man with the heart of a lion and the body of a lion. Eustace.

The mother, the one who knew first that they had found her. Isabella.

Sybilla, the girl who was found.

The river.

SHE WAS FOUND

'They have found her.'

They had found her.

The girl was found.

*

They could stop waiting.

They could stop looking.

She was found.

PART I

WHEN SHE WAS LITTLE

CHAPTER I

I see him standing there. I see him holding her up. I see the shadows that they make, the large round beneath the small. An Orion and a pole star. A man holding up his daughter. A man with shoulders as wide as a railway bridge holding a small child high over his head.

Behind them the sky is lit because today the day is beautiful, because today the river is bright because the sun is bright. The pair is a silhouette, a paper silhouette, traced in relief against the river-bright sky. Behind him the farm and the fields. Beyond him the sea and the cliffs. Below him the little house and the flagstones and a rocking-horse. I see his head and it is up and back. I see hers and it is tilting forward. There is a squeal, of joy it must be, of joy. There is a bellow of pride.

You are a gift from the Gods.

An angel.

You belong among the stars, my angel, among the stars.

I wonder how he feels but I do not need to wonder because it is there to be seen, because he says it with his gestures, with the flamboyance of his mane, with the bounce of his roar. I see that his huge heart aches, I can feel it, almost hear it. His big paws itch. I see, I can feel how he wants the real paw that lies inside the big paw to come out, to be freed so he can touch his daughter and not risk a scratch with his great claw on her divine, heaven-sent, brand-new face. Now he is King Kong. She is the tiny blonde and he holds her high before his huge, tall chest. Swings her round. Shows her to everyone. Shows her to all the other beasts in the jungle and says look what I have, she is mine, I made her, we made her, she belongs among the stars, she is a gift from the gods.

I see him again and it is the same, the man holds high his little girl. Now it is the city that watches him, watches them and I feel him, as he swirls, nimble, powerful, hot in his love, swelled by his love, his breath on fire, his soul on fire, his pride and his chest swollen with hot. And his heart, big beast's as it is, is pounding, the walkways by the river are rising and falling to the beat, the river ruffles to the beat, the warehouses on the far side slip and slide, stick their toes into the foreshore and brace themselves lest this unheralded turbulence unseats them, brings them hurtling into the water. And across the jungle of the city, across the deep dark pull of the river, there is silence because the pride of this man in his daughter, the love of this man for his daughter rings loud.

Every day, this feeling, every day.

CHAPTER II

I look back, further. I see myself, a soon-to-be mother going into labour, face pale, eyes wide, the knuckles that I wrap around the wrist of the soon-to-be father clenched, the skin down my neck red, the space between my shoulder-blades braced, the skin, all my skin, taut and ready to be released, the noise in my ears a mix of blood and roar, my trepidation almost visible, my excitement likewise, almost visible.

I see that in this picture there is a perhaps a hint, a doubt and I remember because how could I forget, because would it be good enough, could I be good enough, could we both be good enough, could everything change, could we not go back, could we lose what we had, could we?

I remember how all that year while we waited, our hearts flowed over, our hearts were bursting, knowing a baby was coming, knowing it was all we both wanted and needed, knowing it was the sum of us, the sum of our love. I remember how day by day passed and each one was brief and each one was precious while we scurried about, getting things, doing things, moving out of the falling-down building that was not ours to live in, moving into a room that Julieta offered us at a cut-price rate, a chambre de bonne she called it, part of Julieta's house but not. Trying to keep our smiles down. Trying to keep our bellows of joy inside our chests while we plotted and tickled. Making the chambre de bonne nice, as nice as we could, pulling off the rest of the wallpaper, scrubbing the green stain from the inside of the bath, making the sink taps not drip, making the cracked sink not leak, making something that could double for curtains out of my student costumes, dragging up a chair we found by the Victorian pumping station, a table. Lying down on the bed side by side and watching our hopes as they rose up inside me, as they wriggled inside me. That long year, that fleeting year and then we were ready, everything was ready and Julieta had come all the way up the stairs with the help of her stick and given us a shawl, one she said she could still remember seeing pinned out when she was a child on the camomile lawn in the shadow of the great house where she herself had been born.

I remember as we went to the hospital and gradually it changed, even as were on the way, excitement was there for sure but so too was this small thin whisper of alarm, what if, what if, what if. Joy and hopes jostled with the whisper and Eustace drove me, then carried me, then wheeled me and it was something I had longed for, something I had dreamt of since I was a girl, something I knew I was destined for, to be a mother, to hold in my arms my daughter, my son, to be one but not one, two, to be three, to be loved from above and also from within, and I should have been somehow in some way full of that, the knowledge that all that was about to become true and real.

We hurtled down the corridor and plunged into a room and there was no stopping, no breathing, no time to wait or think or shout out stop, please wait and time became blackness and whiteness, just those. A day of labour and a night. A day of blackness, a night of whiteness, another day of blackness. The child was coming. The child was not. Between the waves and the surges, I could not think, was I afraid, was I not afraid, no, petrified, was I petrified, no, not petrified, no, caught on the edge of, caught in the middle of, caught in the roundabout of, the merry-go-round of and was there an arrow and did it point in both directions and could I have chosen which way to take, could I? The child was not going to come, it was not going to have life, it was going to have life but I would fail it, we would fail it, yes there would be arrows, an arrow but we would miss it, we would spin past, we would try to hold the wheel and change the spin, I would try and I would not see it, in this day and night and day that were so black and white and black and so, so long. And the nurses too, the doctor, would they help me catch the arrow, take the right way, I did not know, they crowded round the bed and said things and Eustace was pushed away to the side while they did things and sometimes silence came.

CHAPTER III

A week or longer later, when Sybilla had arrived after all, safely after all, when three long days of it were behind us and the exhaustion after that, mother and daughter, when we had both been allowed to go home and Eustace had shipped us in his arms up the narrow steep stairs that were lined with narrow steep half-gloss-painted walls, that smelt of cold stone and no light and nothing shared, then laid us down on the bed and I saw him with eyes wet and I saw him with a hand over his mouth to hide his feelings.

A week or longer later and there was triumph, a faint glow of triumph, I lay there in the tiny bed in the tiny flat and lack of sleep ransacked me, besieged me but still, she was here, I need not have doubted, it was fine. Silence settled and we sank into the bed and waited. Joy was ours because she had been grasped, prised from the wheel of fortune, held safe.

She was small, that was all it was, she was small. As the weeks came and the months, months-and-months, she was still small. We waited. I waited. Sybilla had struggled to be born and now she too seemed to be waiting. In her tininess, in her fragileness, in her uncrying, in her ungrowing, in her coughs that were so slight, I was not even sure they were coughs or if it was my own heart, tick-er-ty ticking as it prayed and hoped for a change in the wind.

Months and then almost a year and it was short and it was long, it was precious and it was instantly lost, each moment of hope superseding the last, squeezing out all memory. Did she smile then? Did she laugh? Was she bigger? When I laid her on Eustace in the dip of his chest, I pictured the time when it would not be so marked, their difference in size, when she would be standing tall against his side, up to his hands maybe, up to his waist, and they would walk together, run together, swing, he pushing, she pushed, her hair brushing his face, her feet going higher even than him.

Mostly it was me, it had to be me. Now and again I saw Eustace look over to us. I saw the look that he had hidden under his hand, the look that said he wanted to be Tarzan or King Kong, wanted to pull out all his real paws from inside his lion's paws, wanted to roar and rampage round the jungle with pride, a look that was made of waiting and hoping and big man and helpless man and man-not-woman and father-not-mother. I saw the look, I smiled, I plunged my anchor into the silt and held onto our child. I imagined myself turning back to look across to him, my hand to my forehead, I could say Ahoy, I could wave Ahoy, I needed his strength, I wanted him but I could not see him because I did not look across at him but drove down inside myself, because above all then I was a mother and above all then she needed me, she was still small, life was hers but only in filigree, only in atoms.

CHAPTER IV

Years later and I recall those months again – it is now and Sybilla has been lost for five years, more than five years, less, she has evaporated, lifted, faded, flattened, curled into the day like smoke, she is here, she is not, she is gone and I am sitting on the bench by the river where he found me with the old cannon pointing east and the stories. How had I felt in those days, when she was little and I was holding on? Were there seasons, was there day, was there night, did dreams, did whispers, did cries, did hands, did holding on? Did holding on? Did we walk along the river as we had in the beginning and she lay between us, in the crook of my arms or his, her tiny form the glue that bound us tighter still, tighter still? Did I ask him, did I say Eustace, what if this is wrong, what if we are failing? Did he reach his hand to my ear, fold the hair behind it, thumb, forefingers, smile at me, lean into me, bathe me in him? The day she has been found and now I look back. All the days, I look back. Perhaps I can recall the exhaustion or the boredom or the not-boredom, the relentless hurtle. Perhaps I can recall how I found a magnifying glass one day, mother-of-pearl handle, one day in Eustace's things when he was out buying cheese and bread, bread and cheese, some fish perhaps, I would not even have noticed and I picked it up in my free hand and held it to the baby's face, to this baby who seemed so reluctant to seize life, to seize me, and I looked at her, in the large. Everything I saw on that day with the magnifying glass foretold life. Sybilla – in the cells of her skin, in the pores that barely existed, in the dust on her eyelashes, in the dew on her lips, in the minimal fair sprigs of hair that lay against her temples ready to sprout – was poised. I saw, I was certain, that Sybilla was a being-in-action. I saw the blood in her capillaries. I could almost see the oxygen in her blood. I could almost see the bones thickening and the sinew stretching and the brain adding cells and this was good, this was promising, yes I can remember that discovery, that feeling, that the magnifying glass had told me the future, that Sybilla and life, they would join, that life did want her after all.

But if I remember that, I also remember the following moments, when I put down the fat bulging glass and it swivelled on the table, rocking back and forth, into the seconds, out of them and I looked at her again and she was still small and I could still hear the echo of that whisper.

CHAPTER V

One night Eustace stood up from the corner of the bed where I lay, where we lay and I saw him go to the front door that had two side-by-side panes of crinkled glass and a letterbox with no cover so the wind blew in and I saw him turn the key in the lock and leave the flat, closing the door behind him with the quietest of clicks.

The building made no sound. His footsteps made no sound. There was no sound. There were no cats and no foxes and owls did not hoot and I lay there and felt the river – which he loved as now he surely loved his daughter – hold him. I pictured him walking as though over the grave of a girl whose life he already sanctified. I saw the river move past him. I heard the city sleep and he put his hands in his pockets and his face inside some big scarf or other, perhaps that embroidered pashmina he had claimed from the belongings left by his mother, and he and his stealth and his wishes and love that was bigger than a jungle's echo marched the banks, on the one bank eastward, on the other to the west.

In the morning, when he opened the door again and re-closed it with the quietest of clicks, when he tiptoed into the room and over to the bed, we were lying the one on the other. Dreamlike sequences of river life spooled past him and into the room. A swan, coots, a boat tipping, another. At one point, a woman stood poised to jump over a parapet into the river. I saw it, as he hovered over us, as we lay eyes closed, hunting sleep, and Eustace talked her down, words less than sounds, tears, the calumny, the gnawing slowness of the minutes.

Mostly, he said when I asked him, there had been nothing. The reach of the river. The years ahead of him that he thought then were unconquerable. The groan of this thing inside him, the chasm.

He began to go every night, while I stayed and nursed Sybilla, while I clung to hope and her tiny body, while I counted her heartbeats and lay as still as my breathing would allow. Eustace's night walks became a solace to him, he said, they helped him fill in the space that had opened up, the space he could not fill because he was a father not a mother, because he loved her more than he could say, because in his mind as he walked through the night, he could feel her hand in his, he could hear her steps three to his one, he could feel her small legs upon his shoulders, he could hear her gurgles of pleasure, he could imagine them daisy-chaining their way through all the nights, through all the time. I would lie there and listen as he flipped down the stairs, opened the door with its slanting-backwards high-pitched hinges, turned left at the bottom and slipped into the night. I pictured him as he walked, eating the pavements, eating the muffled miles, moving through the cushion of the night until he came to the set of steep stone steps that led to the river's foreshore and if the tide was half-out, he went and stood waist-deep in her, waist-deep. I could picture him, from all this way, Eustace in the river, Eustace in the cold and the pull, Eustace filling his mind.

I longed for Eustace and forgot him. In my hands, my arms, pressed against my bosom, this being lay. Maybe a snuffle now and again, maybe an infinitesimal squirm, maybe the flutter of an eyelid that by now, to me, with all this waiting had become so loud, I was sure Eustace would hear it however many river miles away he may have been. Sleep – the drug of forgetting – pulled at me. I felt myself at some points almost ready to follow Sybilla. Perhaps I could be small, like her, and I could disappear down inside until all I was was a form, like her. We could float side by side, sink side by side into that vortex that seemed so close, and then maybe I could take her hand in mine and it would fit and I could look up and holding her, kick my toes and together we could rise through the eddies.

Eustace would be wandering the city, his shadow stalking him through the night haze, that King Kong waiting. I saw his shadow as there was no light, no shadow and I saw him reach over, his strong arms and he would catch us and pull us free.

I leaned back into the pillows. I did not think, I did not dare, about the future. There was no future. There was only now. To keep myself from falling off, I dipped now and again into the shallows of my past, winding memories, old stories around myself, winding them around Sybilla because maybe if she knew the past, if she heard the thrum of it, the hymn of it, if she felt the whispers of the people that had come before her breathe through her hair, maybe she would see something. Maybe it would glimmer and beckon her. She would rise up, she too would kick, we would break through the eddies.

One day Eustace came up the stairs – burst in through the rickety door, back from a night-walk but later than usual, later – and he had a parcel.

'A present, my darling love.'

It was wrapped in brown paper and I could not open it because she was in my arms so I asked him and when he tore off the paper, there was the face of a clock. It had been a grandfather clock, he said, but the case had long since gone and now it was just the face and the mechanism. The moon painted with pink cheeks and wide eyes and a smile, the stars with delicate, swooping lashes and Alice-in-Wonderland grins. I handed him Sybilla so I could pick it up. I held it before me. Looked at it as though it was a mirror. I smiled at its smile and winked at its lashes. I put it on the old tea-chest that we used for a bed-side table, the one marked Ceylon and while he sat at the end of the bed cradling her, bending his neck into the shawl, I sat again among the pillows and gave myself to the rhythm of this strange, wonderful thing.

And at the same time asked myself how many circuits the hands would do before Sybilla joined us, before once and for all she chose life.

PART II

OH THOSE DAYS

CHAPTER I

Where did we meet? At art college? Yes it must have been at art college. It must have been when I was a life model and he was one of maybe twenty students, his rum-dark hair curtaining his eyes as he leant into the easel, his arm cramped to his side and a pencil and a sheet of brown wrapping paper, his choice, and his powerful electric silence. I remember him then, I do, he was not etiolated like the others, he was not patchwork, his intensity was not assumed, it hung all around him.

Or maybe it was not actually in the art college. Maybe it was at the chip van that stopped on the corner of the street outside the college and he was buying saveloy and I was standing back, wondering, should it be chips, should it be peas and chips, should it be peas..

Both of the above are possible. I remember the van and I can still taste the bitter fatty smell of the batter and the air around us on the corner of that street outside the college. I remember the life class and him, how he drew in great sweeps, wiped those sweeps with his sleeve, drew again, banged his pencil on the easel shelf, then threw it across the room, then went to pick it up, then snapped it. I remember that he did not talk, he did not gambol, he did not suck himself in before spouting Baudelaire. He came and went. He drew and left.

Perhaps we met for real that time when I saw him months later, long after I had given up being a life model, when I was all dresses, nothing but dresses, nothing but doubloons and bodices, ribbons and frogs, and there one day coming out of his school was Mister Coldwinter, walking in big trousers, wading through the shoals of little boys who were his pupils. There were cast-iron gates with wrought pillars that finished in the shape of fuchsias. There was the courtyard beyond that, between us. There was the school door and it was break-time and he was in front of the door and the boys were around him, squealing. Did I shout out hello? Did I wave? Did I even catch his eye?

Or was it that afternoon when I was walking in the park in the summer, hibiscus here, anemones there, the grass parched, the people splayed. At the time I had a fluffy dog and I was marching. Through the people. Past the flowers. And there he was, alone, a tartan woollen blanket on the brown cracked ground beside him while he was on his knees, leaning over a bush, getting as close as he could to the butterflies, the peacocks and painted ladies that were fluttering there.

Perhaps we would always meet, it would never be a real chance encounter, it would be as if some deity had moved us, plotted it, Pawn to A3 takes King.

CHAPTER II

Afterwards, he told me, after we had crossed paths enough times, he decided to leave his job at the school. He could not do art, it turned out, not the way his college thought it should be done, not the way they proscribed it, pads and easels and subject matter that was mannered and too much indoors. He could teach this kind of art and he did, but he said it was not him, it was constrained and he was not, at least not inside. He said it made his soul shrink and afterwards I thought he must have meant the opposite, that his soul was bursting out, banging against the side of his ribs until he could no longer bear it.

'Decided to leave. Risky. But decided anyway.'

He took me through the day of his leaving the school and we were walking along the river and it was the first time. Managed to tell the headmaster politely, he said, that he could no longer stay, thank you very much, been marvellous, loved every minute, sorry and all; managed to walk out of the building that was built around a five-storey caged lift shaft without skipping or singing or cheering or punching the air or spelling out Hallelujah with his tongue on the frost in the courtyard; managed not to look back while the small faces he had taught crowded at a window, watched him go, eyes crammed together like frog-spawn; managed to walk down the street without doing star jumps, without whistling, without swirling round old ladies that were trundling past; managed to hold direction, hold true, go on the right road, along to somewhere he thought I would be, he was sure he had seen me there before, which I was, on the bench, by the river, looking east, my breath making pools of mist in front of me, the old cannon silent alongside; managed not to make it all go wrong, he said, when he said hello, when he said his name, you remember we met, when he said would you like to walk the river with me.

And then we were walking and he was telling me this and all the things, making me laugh, he said, making me smile, making me skip along beside him even though my boots were too big round my ankles. Managed to ask me if I would do it again, walk again with him and I said yes, I would do it again and this time, we went further, it was hazy, still cold and we could have been figments of some troubled, strange imagination, dim figures wandering mistily through the late night blur.

Managed to take me as far as the boatyard on only the second time of our walking where he showed me the big old coal-barge, hanging out of the water she was, on a crane. Stood behind me, reached one arm over my shoulder, round in front of me, placed his hand under my chin, tilted my head gently up so I could see her as she was, Ann of Goole. Ann of Goole he said into the ear that was closest to his mouth, the full length of her, the full one-time glory of this great river-going behemoth. Ann of Goole and with one hand still on my chin and the other on my waist, on the other side, gentle, he whispered into my ear the stories he pictured, of the men on board, of the dirt, of the coal, the grain, the wool, the dark, the rock and roll; told me how she sprang from the tradition of the longships, her years passed plying inland rivers, delivering vast cargoes that were well beyond the horses, onto the lighters, onto the quays; told me how she moved and all things fell aside to let her past, told me how she sat on the water and all things looked up to her, told me one day, whispering in the same ear while my head tipped back towards his, he too would be a sea stallion, a dragon Harald, he said, he would sell his own liver if he had to, he would work till his limbs were raw if he had to, he would take himself apart plate by plate, sell himself rivet by rivet if he had to, work all day and all night and all life until he could buy this barge, have this barge; and then after he had bought her, he would take her apart plate by plate and put her back together again plate by plate with his bare hands and his bare will, working till he bled if he had to, holding steel and rope and net and flame and wax within his teeth, if he had to.

Managed to keep his poise – and he paused when he whispered this – while he stood back from behind me, came to stand beside me, put his hand deep in his pockets and looked straight ahead, not at me, at the river, not at the river, into his hopes while he confessed, it was a confession, I see that now if I could not see it then, the mist, the pounding mist, told me he was young, told me he had no money, only dreams.

Managed to convince her when he said, Isabella what's your surname, that one day, one day she would be his.

CHAPTER III

Those days and we had nothing. His dreams and the nursing of his dreams. Those days and after miles of the river and miles of the city, after hours of shared silence, just the matched cadenced passage of our footsteps while we ran in and out of arcades and closes, inspecting everything that was there to be seen. The river and we re-made her, the wharf buildings that were going, those that were gone, the foreshore, the tides, the locks, the river wall. Feet in the cold swirl and we put our elbows on our knees and our chins in our hands. Feet on the hard and we moved inwards, looked at churches, looked at banks and cinemas, privies and coal-sheds, statues and graveyards. We walked parks, we walked pavements. We read things, plaques and headstones, and studied things, a curve here, a finial there, admired things, scoffed at things, learnt, devoured. We lay down and made colours. We sat up and stood up and ran and saw the colours, everywhere. We sang and in our mind the song was the city and the song was the river. We spoke and the words trailed us, droplets in our wake. We shouted out and the words overtook us and they grew into bubbles and into more songs and into the colours we had made.

The river held us and one day, it was even colder now, we found a high Georgian tenement squeezed almost to one window's width between some Victorian terraces, the high Georgian tenement empty, dilapidating out of anyone's ken and we climbed in, over the back wall, through the back hedge and he pushed the door and I slid past him and walked inside.

Those days and when we were not walking, we began patrolling the story of our new hide. No one came there, it was as though it did not exist except for itself, this wonderful Georgian beauty. It did not exist except for us so we spread ourselves about in it, sometimes shouting up to the cupola – it was oblong and divided into petals, its glass a greeny white – at the top of the staircase, just for the joy of hearing our shouts echoing back, just for the joy of reminding ourselves that no-one else knew we were there. Eustace had just enough money that we could eat and we ate in that tall blue house, moving from one room to the next, climbing over one hole in the floor to the next, balancing on one exposed beam, then another. Bread and sometimes cheese and bread. Cheese and bread and sometimes cheese and bread and wine. While we danced. While we sat down on the floorboards and played absent-mindedly with the frayed ends of the wallpaper. While we cleared circles with the heels of our hands on the windowpanes so we could look out into the battered wilderness garden which the house hid in its shadow. While we went down into the garden and stood under the tangled tree and looked up through it, me leaning against him, he standing behind me. While we threw our heads right back and laughed. While we raced each other up and down the stairs until one day the banister toppled with a crash into the ground floor hallway. While we lay on our makeshift bed on the floor and looked up through the holes in the roof. While we danced. There was a stove – cast-iron, pot-bellied thing that croaked if you lit it – and we lit it and we sprawled out on one of his tartan rugs, for he had a collection, and listened to the croaking and listened to each other's breathing and made promises that we both knew for sure even then, even in that house that was falling down around us when we were both nothing, we would never break.

'Do you have sisters?' I asked and I knew before he answered – while he cartwheeled his fingertips along the top of my arm, down my wrist, along my waist – that he was alone.

CHAPTER IV

Oh those days and how we talked. How we painted in our stories, how we drew them on the bare plaster walls, on the white dirty floorboards, in the air that was lit with dust. I took him to that faraway place of my childhood and the shells on the shore and the mussels on the ropes and the heather on the moor to the south, behind us and the blackcock, every now and again, the blackcock. I took him and walked the bounds of early holidays, said hello to the man who clipped the tall beech hedges of the big house, said hello to the man who lived in the cabin on the shore looking plumb north into the eyes of the aurora when it came. Spoke to my grandmother who was knitting socks, always knitting socks, four needles as though it was just that easy.

'Grandmother, shall we go and see the plovers?'

and Eustace's head rolled to the side to watch me, lying flat we both were, as I mimicked the tongue of my grandmother, how it ran along her top lip, rising and falling as it came across the long black hairs that sprouted there.

'Please can we go and see the plovers?'

and at last, I told him, my grandmother put down her work, huffed, stopped her rocking, stood up from the crinoline chair in the old kitchen with the range sputtering smoke and whistled through her two front teeth:

'Well come on then, Isa, take my hand, what are you waiting for?'

There was colour on that north shore, in that story I was telling him, in the visits to the woman who was the mother of my mother, who knitted socks and sold them to the islands, who knew someone who knew someone who remembered meeting Bonnie Prince Charlie. Navy blue outline of a woman in a smock and big boots, thin but wiry. Navy blue because that was as bright as she would go, being Scottish, being a 'hard-nut Highlander' as she called herself. Being as I found out when I was older, a member of the Free Church, a worshipper of a God that was if not unforgiving, at least austere, a worshipper of abstinence, of frugality, of lace collars but only on a high day. Silhouette in paler blue of a girl also in a smock but her too-big boots smaller, her hand enclosed in the thin wiry hand that was more often wrapped around a skein of three-ply. Light of the sun on the shore, as they walked, bouncing off the water in great yellow discs that dazzled them. Bronze-green of the marsh grass as it blew in the wind that always stroked this shore. Distant glittering specks of the plovers, bob-bob-bobbing in the shallows. Bob-

bob. Something scared the birds as woman and child grew close and as one, the flock lifted. And the drops of sea-water, I said to him while he lay next to me on the floor with his head turned to mine, falling from the plovers' feet, catching the sun like bits of glass. The birds were in a cloud of themselves, wings and feathers and flying and they too sparkled or shone or glowed and the sky was so blue it made my eyes ache and then they swooped and I raised my head up high to watch them – and I told him, I could still feel it, the warmth of my grandmother through her dark blue hard-nut Highlander tunic, her thin knees and her warmth.

And then when we were on our way back and we passed the little shed that belonged to the big house with the beech hedges that the old man kept clipped year-round and grandmother said – as she always did – 'that's where the Jacobites hid their treasure, wooden chests higher than your head, coins more than a man could count in a day'. And I pictured him, Bonnie Prince Charlie, with brand new socks digging in the shed to find his gold.

Then it would be his turn and I asked him to say but mostly he could not. It was not Scotland, that much I knew, in spite of the blankets. It was a small town, he said, somewhere, nowhere. It was this city, he said, here by the river. There was no grandmother, he said, there was no man of the hedges. He had no memories, he said, none that counted.

CHAPTER V

How long did we stay in the cupola palace with the holes and the tangled tree and the no-longer banister? How long did we have that time when there was no one else, no neighbour or friend or intrusion or kink in the road or need or gaping mouth to come between us? I sit here now and think of those days and paint them, draw them, write them, intertwine them with the older stories, prose them and poem them, red them and white them, weave them, knit them, stitch them and hem them and wear them. Today she has been found and I am sitting here with him and not with him, beside him and it is possible that in finding her, we might lose one another. And yet we have this, the cloak and shawl and pashmina, the elixir of those days.

In the sketch in my mind on the bare plaster wall of the blue Georgian house, to the infinitely gargantuan, soul-bursting, heart-bursting leonine packet of life that lay beside me, to the promise of love that wrote itself out in huge capital letters across everywhere we looked, we painted the nights away, sparks of light swimming around the sea-dark stars.

PART III

AT THE END OF THE RIVER

CHAPTER I

Of course, just as we could not stay in the dilapidating Georgian tall blue house when we discovered I was having a baby, no more could we stay in Julieta's chambre de bonne when we no longer had money, when the ingots he had saved up from the envelopes he was given every week while he was Mister Coldwinter in the school with the corduroy boys had been used up. Julieta said she did not want us to leave because Eustace was her favourite tenant in all her forty-five years of lodgers, because she loved him as one of her own, so much so that she even forgave him for spinning her cat Lady Grace until she thought the cat would disappear in a wheel of flame, but she could not afford to keep us, she was old and frightened about money herself.

We knew snippets of Julieta's story from the photographs she had on a lower bookshelf, from the whiffs of grandeur that blew out of her and across our bows. We knew parts of her story too from moments when she told it to us, when she dared to look back, when she brought out one of her ivory glove-stretchers, her shagreen jewellery box, the buttons with the same crest, the sheets with the same initials stitched into the corners. It was a broken jigsaw but all the same, we knew enough to understand that what she said was real, that her fear was real, that the camomile lawn had not been a metaphor, that the old castle she had lived in and the old ways she knew had slipped away so easily, so disastrously that her fear about more slipping away was probably as three-dimensional to her as the aspidistra that sat on her window-ledge and the sun-bleached pianola that half-blocked up her hall.

*

The pigeon that roosted in the plane tree opposite the door that led onto the street by the river was there when they left and it watched a small trinity that looked like refugees or poor pilgrims, a woman, an infant, a man and there were two bags and though the pigeon did not know it, one of them contained not just clothes and tartan rugs but the moon-and-stars clock and a ready-to-reassemble version of the tea-chest marked Ceylon.

CHAPTER II

Looking back years later, I see those early days with Eustace and Sybilla – when there was no money for a house on the river – in shades of haze, maybe muslin, maybe toile. Hazy the exhaustion that we both felt, he from the work and I from the caring for a child about whom I could not stop worrying even when asleep. Hazy blue and then at times hazy green, when we worked on a harvest together perhaps, loading bales onto trailers and Sybilla would be on his back in a papoose or in a basket under a tree and there would be this thing that we shared, a common goal, common sweat, bones as weary as one another's. From farm to farm, from boat to boat.

We had headed that day from Julieta's to the end of the river, to the point where it joined with the sea. It was Eustace's idea, there was land there, there were orchards and fields, there were farms. He had always known the river, always. He would do anything, he said, and he did – nets and buckets and boats' bottoms and gates and sheds and tractors. Anything. Hazy grey and we lay there at night, in a little cottage, more like a shed at the far end of the river with no track and hardly a roof and windows choked with ivy, and talked more about the things that had made us: my Highland beginnings with the light from the north and all those stories lying about in ruined crofts and big houses where no one lived because it was all too hard by then; his only childness, his early orphanness, his non-parent rememberingness, the mystery of his past that followed him round like a sack of coal, a black coaly sack of nothing.

Sometimes I lost myself again on that north coast, feeling again my grandmother's hand or the bite of the sea wind or the crunch of the heather under our feet as we made our way back to top up the range with peat. The sky that proved beyond all doubt the world was round because it came right down to your ankles, only it did not but slipped over the horizon full of cut-glass sparkles that may have been the plovers or may have been their cousins, the peewits. Feeding my grandmother's stock, her few sheep, her Highland cows. Learning their names and then calling their names, not being frightened when they ran towards us even though I knew they could knock me over because they had, twice before. Walking along the side of the burn and trying not to fall in while I made her tell me about the old times, about the crofts that had been there and the families. A summer picnic by the lighthouse on the top of a rock with a hard-boiled egg each and some oatcakes and the noise of the kittiwakes in their colony below and guillemots streaking past us at eye level.

And then years later when I went back, when my grandmother was ill and in the hospital, so small, half-finished sock on the table by her bed but she could not touch it or see me, she was blind now and half way on her journey back to the Lord; and I sat and held her hand which wore one of the pairs of mittens she had knitted and not sold. And a few days after that, when the frugality and self-denial of a lifetime had finally been realised and she had been gathered, she had drifted off to the place where there is hardly any food and you only wear lace collars on a high day; and when some men in big coats who did not smile had scooped what was left of her, plus a full set of needles, into the plain box, no brass; and when her tiny bones rattling in the box had been dropped into that part of the graveyard where the rocks are deeper; and when the dirt had been crumbled on top of her, I went to pack up her things in her cottage. The wind was low, around my ankles. The sky was everywhere, grouse cackling and I saw the place, I saw the beauty, how raw it was, how tough she must have been, this wiry human person who had taught me without teaching me, living there at the very edge of the world where the soldiers that this land had bred had enjoyed a reputation of bloodiness and fearlessness because of course they would, they were hewn from granite.

In our river's-end cottage with its peeping eyes, between days of labour, between the hazes, now and again I asked Eustace to take a turn.

'Now it's your turn. Tell me of your father. Did you see the birds with him, did you walk the fields with him, did he have a fine chest, buggers' grips, a long beard, a belly, did he smoke, take snuff, take whisky, smell of goat, smile with his eyes, show you things, shoot a rabbit, skin a rabbit, catch a fish, catch a ball, throw a ball?'

'And your mother? Was her hair long, were her dresses long, were they velvet or linen, were they waisted or straight or gathered round the shoulders, did she even wear dresses or just smocks, and if she wore just smocks, what colour, how long and did she read to you, talk to you, spit on a hankie to rub the blood off your knees, trim your fringe, fluff your fringe, call you anything, my treasure, my tiger, my lion, hold you on her lap, take you on walks with her and your small hand was in hers, cry when you went to school on that first day, cry when you cried, cry when you laughed?'

He did not mind the questions, he did not seem to mind the questions, in fact I saw him smile when I said smell-of-goat, smile as he was made to look back, move his hand to his smile, pause a moment, pause. But all he could say in reply was that he could not remember, it had all gone, his parents had left him behind as soon as they could, taken a train, taken a boat, left him with an aunt or several, left him. Taken his memories. Taken it all.

And then he burst up from lying to sitting as though he were Gulliver breaking the threads of the Lilliputians. He burst up, joked me, laughed me, swore me, ruffled me, growled me, dazed me and I suppose he thought that then I would not notice, would I, that he spoke uniquely of the future, the boat we would buy, the work he would do, the things he would make with his hands and his iron will, the hopes that he had for us all, this little unit of ours, Sybilla taking her place in the stars where she belonged, me working beside him, with him while we built a universe that would be the envy of even those who had no dreams. That he did not speak of the past. That he did not.

One day perhaps, I wondered, would he talk about this, beyond the dreams and the future and the unit and the stars and the boat and the things he would make, would there be no pause, would there be no smile, would there be no no-past, no no-parents? Or would he never, because he never had, he never would, because to look back at a blank page of memory was too hard, because he was King Kong, he was Tarzan, because he was a lion and the coaly sack of nothing was just a familiar.

CHAPTER III

'Hat-Man.'

It was the first word, Sybilla's first word, the child had spoken, she had said something, it was a word. We had been there for a year. We had been there for two. We were thin, we were tanned, we were fit, we were exhausted, we were together.

'Hat-Man.'

Eustace was with her, I was outside, it was he who heard it first and he picked her up, wrapped his arm around Sybilla's waist, scooped her under his chin and ran and I saw him coming, looked like he was holding a hand-grenade with the pin out, only in a good way, in a joyous way and he ran along the flagstones and into the farmyard and he shouted out, in a kind of shout that was trying not to be too loud,

'Isabella. Isabella!'

'Hat-Man. Hat-Man.'

Sybilla said it again. She said it again and again and again. I was stitching. On the bench, in the thickening dusk. I was lost in it, the motion of my fingers, the dreams those motions made, the thing of beauty that this piece of cloth and those few slender threads would make when I was done. Eustace bounced towards me, arm round Sybilla. I saw that his hands were thickened, no longer the hands that held a pencil by an easel. Isabella, he said, and he sat down in the sun on the stone bench next to me and he sat her at our feet on an old jacket that he had been wearing while he worked and together we watched her at the side of the cottage with the view of the fields that fell into the sea just like hope.

'Hat-Man.'

She was still small for her age, still at a remove from the world, still coated in silence for the most part, an anomaly and yet everything, all our thoughts. It was a spring day, it was a March day, the sparrows were arguing in the honeysuckle on the side of the shed-house, the celandines were poking their yellow umbrellas up through the cracks in the flagstones and Sybilla had come out of her shell, on this day of so many days of waiting, pecked a hole not with tears, not with cries, not with screams of rage or hunger or tiredness but with this word, this six-letter word which only she had made because neither of us had ever, we were sure, said anything that sounded remotely similar.

This must be a good sign, we said, no an amazing sign, no a completely absolute upside down reversal of what we had expected. That Sybilla can talk, that

Sybilla has a word. It is not strange, this word, we said, it is not odd that this is the only word. She has a word, she has a voice, she may not be following it up with Mummy or Pappa or anything but she has a word.

I put my hand on Eustace's knee on that bench in that sunshine and did not dare to look at him or catch his eye or even feel his knee in my palm although I must have gripped it as though it were an ice-axe. I thought of the dandelions I had blown with a wish, wishing her to become real, the times I had closed my eyes while holding her and begged the superior being to let her be alive, fighting for life, fighting for me when I opened them again. I thought of the times I had laid her down in the drawer we used as her crib and felt her like lace in my fingers as I let her go and longed for the moment to come when the drawer would have to be substituted for a whole chest of drawers, for a wardrobe. I thought of all that silence she had brought with her, the cotton wool that filled our days with her, the ear-muffs we felt we were wearing during all those early years of her because hardly ever, hardly ever did she make a sound.

And now this. It was as though lead crystal glasses were falling downstairs. It was as though spring was made for this. It was as though the moon-and-stars clock had been waiting for this. Eustace picked her up from the old jacket – after she had said her word a hundred, two hundred times – and he cupped his hands in her armpits and he raised her, and I could feel him, I could hear him inside, here she was, at last poking through, the daughter, the 'Jane', the treasure he had longed to hold up and claim as his, made by him, made by us, King to A3 takes Pawn. All the spades and the wheelbarrows and the things he used in this relentless physical life we had adopted just for now, picking fruit, picking vegetables, mending fences, feeding stock, going to the water, mending the boats, scraping the boats and I knew he wanted to run to the top of the highest hill and take the word and hold it up, before he held her up, before he stood like the man and the child cut out against the backdrop of a southeast sea. He would shout out, hold her up against his chest or place her on his back like he was a primate and she was his primate infant, exclaim because at last, because at last Sybilla had returned from wherever it was she had been.

'Hat-Man.'

We heard her say it again and again. Hat-Man and Eustace. I saw him, holding her up, holding the word, Eustace, and his tears that were like night-time leaf-fall, quiet and forever.

That night we sat at the table which was not a table, it was a crate and the moon-and-stars clock watched us and we watched it. He said out loud four years, five months, two days. He put his head right ear down, eyes looking at nothing, although the chair he had made for me out of that yew that I loved was in his line of sight. I could hear his breathing, I could feel his thoughts and we sat together, embraced by the tick, both of us the same, hoping the same, that this was the beginning of the end of the ordeal, that it was receding into years gone by, that the noise of the moon-and-stars clock would become what it always should have been, not a threat from the future but a moments-ago measuring of the past.

CHAPTER IV

There were celandines and aconites and wild orchids and buttercups in the grass that lined the river as it strolled down to the sea. The long cry of the oystercatcher rang out. A dipper flitted over the rocks. On the full moon, woodcock had come and gone. The small ferns that clung to the drystone wall next to the grass alongside the river caught the light in their spores and glimmered. The buds on the ash trees were black still but on the wild cherries, blossom fluttered. The water was calmer, not so much spate, not so much froth and soupy brownness, not so many dead twigs on the surface. Rooks bickered. Seagulls would have stolen our sandwiches if we had had sandwiches. It was that spring – the spring when Sybilla began to join the world.

Just after the calves began to come, Eustace announced that at the end of this one-more summer, one-more harvest, one-more season on the farm making good, in the harbour making good, working all hours, back-breaking, leg-breaking, skin-chafing, this one-more summer lifting bales, stacking bales, sneezing with the pollen, wiping the sweat off our foreheads with the back of our hands leaving long streaks of dark from the dust, we would have enough money, he had saved enough money, we could go back to the top of the river and buy his Ann of Goole.

'I promised you, my angel, I promised you.'

We had to go and help a cow, the farmer came and shouted, and Eustace picked Sybilla up and swung her onto his shoulders for she was almost strong enough now and as she passed his head, he nuzzled her, and then she sat on top and I saw her little hands gingerly make their way through the thick hair, holding on.

'I promised you, my angel, I promised you.'

And after we had come back from calving the cow – a fine bull calf, red as fire – after I had held the rope and he had pulled the rope and Sybilla had sat in the grass and cited Hat-Man a hundred, a thousand times, after we had untied the ropes and made sure the old girl was suckling him, made sure it was all good, after he had remounted Sybilla up on his shoulders and we walked through the spring evening, through the poking-through grass, through the noise of the season growing ripe, after we got back to the little house, Eustace put our daughter back on the old jacket that was now in the kitchen and he went outside somewhere and came back in, pulling behind him from goodness knows where a rocking horse that he had been making all this time. Dappled by his own hand, tacked up and be-ribboned and shod and plaited by his own hand, be-wheeled by his own hand, a hint of pink in the nostrils, a hint of velvet at the muzzle, a saddle studded with red felt and brass, a ride-a-cock-horse bridle, shells on her fingers and bells on her toes, stirrups enclosed at the front by leather so if there was a buck or a squeal, Sybilla's tiny foot would not go through.

He bent forward, rum-dark hair over his eyes, put his hands round her little waist, the dress that I had made and smocked puckering under his grip, and lifted her onto the red-felt and brass-studded saddle. Placed her little feet, one after the other, into the stirrups. Put the reins, one after the other, into her little hands. Gently we wheeled the rocking-horse back out into the garden, onto the dark slate with the celandines between the slabs and the late evening spring sun and the sea barking in the distance and he stood and I stood and we watched while the pony rocked and the little girl held on.

CHAPTER V

Through the last throes of that spring, through the grand blossom of our final summer of working on the farm, through the hard work, through the heat, through the dust and then the rain and then the ruined harvest and then the goodbyes to the farmer, to the shed-house, to that time, we came to know Hat-Man as one of our own.

At times, when Sybilla spoke, it was less often to us than it was to an open space in front of her. She took a forkful of food and presented it to the space, making the same noises of encouragement that I myself was still obliged to make to her. At others, Sybilla was Hat-Man and Hat-Man was Sybilla and then you could not talk to either, neither spoke. In the evenings, Eustace loved to take Sybilla for walks, holding her hand as they skirted the cliffs or the field up the hill behind the cottage and when they got back, I watched him watch her as she bent down and leant into the open space to take off tiny imaginary boots, one by one. Eustace once asked Sybilla – would Hat-Man like to come for a walk with us – but he did not know that they had swapped and for two weeks afterwards, there was no mention of Hat-Man and no tiny boots and no forkfuls. Eustace walked in front of Sybilla – inadvertently – he had burst in from the workshop to tell us his news, his big job news, his now-we-can-go-to-the-city-and-survive news and he did not know, he could not have seen but he planted his great man's farmer boot on Hat-Man and he turned round because a terrible silence was flooding the room and we watched in horror as our daughter deflated like a punctured tyre. She never cried, not even then, not even when he had stood on Hat-Man and she sat with her finger pointing into the open space where Hat-Man should have been but was no longer because he was now just a pool of squashed nothing.

When we packed up the cottage and piled in to the old estate car that Eustace had found abandoned and banged into life, we had to make space on the back seat so she could build a safe place for Hat-Man, 'Here is for Hat-Man'. Hat-Man came with us while we left the tiny shed with the slate floors and the outside loo, while we bumped along the long roads that grew less bumpy as they grew more long, while we moved from the green to the black, from the soft to the hard, from the fields to the big city, out of the estate car and up the narrow stairs and once more into the chambre de bonne.

Julieta was delighted to see us again, she said so, she had known we would come, she had been sure, because we had money now, he had written to her, and she waved her old crone's hand at Sybilla, how she has grown. Julieta was introduced to Hat-Man and from the back of her chair where the cushion had worn down low, she raised herself up and forwards and was very polite. She looked frailer, a little, and she rang a bell and Mrs Cowan, her mother's cook from the old days when they were still in the castle, when stupid people had not thrown it all away, emerged from the pantry at the end of the corridor and brought glasses that were too small for Eustace's hands and we drank sherry.

We had been to the end of the river. We had taken with us only dreams and a silent bundle of girl. We had made new muscles and learnt new forms of endurance and the names of flowers and how to calve and how to walk in the fields and see every little thing, every blow of every blade, every whisper, the carpet of life.

And now we were back. Julieta said I have spent a lot of time remembering, I did not want to let you go. She said to Sybilla you are exactly as I would have pictured, four now, four big years old and your long fair curly hair and your blue-green eyes. She said to Sybilla I am very pleased to meet Hat-Man. She said to us both, to us all, everything is going to be fine and on that day, around that chair, with those glasses and that old sherry that tasted more of age than of grape, we felt like we were standing on tiptoes, ready to dance.

PART IV

EUSTACE'S DREAMS

CHAPTER I

So now. I must have known it, how much Eustace had held this moment in his mind's eye. I must have known it because of the sweat that he poured and the blood that he spilt and the sleep that he did not have. Down on the fields, down in the harbour and sometimes squalls that might make other men buckle, swept aside by Eustace, carved through.

I did know it. We shared it, if not in words, then in passion, then in silent passion, then in nights when we held back sleep so we could discuss it, not with words but with touch. With the eyes of the night peeping through the ivy and I felt him nursing his dreams, stoking up the fire of his dreams, running down the railway track of his single mind until he made it.

And now it is now and we are at the boatyard, the four of us, and it is time.

Eustace was ready, poised in the vertigo of the moment. I stood behind him with Sybilla and Hat-Man in my arms. The man was sitting at his desk and Eustace stood before him. Eustace dropped the red and mustard-gold carpet-bag he carried over his shoulder onto the tooled leather top. He flipped it, tipped it out. There were coins and notes and rolls of notes and the noise smelt of money and the office smelt of men. Counting and the low murmur of counting and the breathiness. Counting again in case they had missed something and the man put the notes into a metal box with a gold rim and he locked it and slowly he shuffled pieces of paper, Eustace ready to bounce up, waiting to bounce up and bellow.

The office-man at the boatyard raised his eyes towards us. In his hand was one piece of paper in particular. He had a dab of tobacco on his top lip and the skin around his nose and his mouth was brown with smuts. He smiled at me, at us, at Sybilla. He wore no side, he wore no baubles or rings, he seemed like just a man – just a man who was once again thousands and thousands of pounds the richer, just a man who would soon be at the Lamb & Flag holding a pint of bitter, waving it about with glee, waving it about like another old salt recently home from months at sea, just a man who would announce to anyone who listened in the Lamb & Flag or wherever else, he said he's going to make her again.

'My arse! She's too far gone for anyone,'

And with that the man would laugh to whoever was listening, from under his cap, from up inside his boots.

Even if Eustace had been in the Lamb & Flag and seen and heard the man's words for himself, he would not have seen and heard them. He was lost already, lost once the coins were counted, lost once the rolls of notes were unrolled and flattened out and patted down, lost once the keys of Ann were in his hand.

'My arse!' he might have said himself but it would have been a beer-swilled roar not of mockery but of joy, my arse, my arse. For now he knew, that he did not just walk away from things like he had from the boys at the school, that the river would be his, that the dreams would be his. He knew because he knew. He knew because he was a man of power, a man of dreams. He knew that the boat would be made whole again, his.

To begin the work, to walk her over, mull her over, think her. To pull her apart plate by plate, bolt by bolt. To pull out all the rottenness. To make this woman large again and proud again, the great icon of the waters that she deserved to be. To lift her down from dry dock. To make her for us. To make us, bond us, hold us. To make a dream. To feel as a man should feel. To see a dream.

We smiled back at the boatyard man. Eustace shook his hand, oblivious to the stories that were about to be told in the pub. He had his new big-job, he had his boat, he had his promises that he had made to me, his promises that he had made to his little girl and we walked the three, four, five of us like kings, kings kongs, the rocking-horse wheeling along in its own version of a dance while the sun caught on the river and bounced on the brass studs of the saddle and bounced on the smile of the little girl and caught on a line of joy that ran down all our cheeks.

From that night, in the chambre de bonne with the moon-and-stars clock and the reassembled tea-chest from Ceylon, Sybilla slept in her own bed, not a drawer, not a wardrobe, her own Eustace-made bed. It was different now. I could breathe. He had his dreams and they were coming.

CHAPTER II

Ann of Goole and yes, from the very next day, Eustace climbed down inside his resolution, throwing himself into the bowels of it. Sparks flew. Splinters flew. Barrows filled with wood to be burnt and wood to be given away. Plates were removed and blasted and replaced. Rust, oh the rust, and the barnacles and the mildewed this and the rotten-through the other. Eustace by day had begun on his big-job, new big-job and he was feverish, working day and day, night and night, no night walks along the river, no stories of my past on the end of our bed while she slept, no rest. He was beginning at the bottom, everything to learn, new techniques, new methods, not drawing now, no sir.

The moon-and-stars clock ticked and its smile was bright and its eyebrows and the lashes of the stars curled as Betty Boopily as they could, as Alice-in-Wonderlandly as they could and a year passed, a whole year. Half way through that year, the front deck had been made safe and so we walked the rocking-horse to the boatyard and rolled the rocking-horse up the steps and in front of the wheelhouse while Ann hung high above, crane-high and Sybilla sat with Hat-Man on the saddle beside her while Eustace – in the leggy, curvey, dappled shadow – bent over, while he banged, while he drilled and welded and drilled again, while he used his teeth and his steel and his promises to put her back together, plate by plate.

Ann of Goole and that summer we all grew brown again, tanned not so much by dust and soil but by light, for the light on her came off the water and bathed us all. Once we brought Julieta. She was worried about leaving Lady Grace but she made it anyway, with her stick and her memories and some Gentlemen's Relish Mrs Cowan had found on a shelf in her kitchenette. We had some bread and some cheese and some wine. I looked at her and thought of my grandmother and how she would disapprove, it was a Sabbath. Julieta said it was like her old castle, only a water castle. She said why don't you grow camomile on the roof in low flat troughs and you can dry your clothes in the sun. She said Sybilla looks fine on her horse today. And Eustace, who up until then had been far away, exhausted or maybe just seeing drill-holes in rows and rows into the future, turned to the old crone and smiled like a god.

Ann of Goole and slowly she took form. No longer a space in front of us or in Eustace's mind or in our far-ahead future but now a shape that could soon be dropped into the water and trusted to float and trusted to look after us, Eustace's unit, to share the river with us and with him. That summer and while he banged, I scraped and Sybilla trotted alongside, piaffed with still few words and still slight, and that still faint but distinct feeling that she would pull away if she could, pull away, she did not cease to pull away. While Hat-Man rode with her, just in front.

CHAPTER III

By the winter, we were ready to move from the chambre de bonne into the water castle. The last few of my costumes I sewed into curtains and bed covers. We brought the table we had found by the pumping-station and the chair and the Ceylon chest and the collection of rugs and the moon-and-stars clock which I hung on the wooden panel above the wheel so that when the boat sailed, we would be going towards time. Our cabin was lined with deep red chintz and folds of racing-green velvet and the odd hint of a sequin. Crewel work from a strange skirt I had once made. Fringes round the top because I had seen that in the old Georgian house under the fallen plaster, black bobbles fluffily festooned at intervals beneath the ceiling.

We would be living not far from Julieta – a river's breadth – but we held a goodbye evening around her pianola. More sherry and Gentleman's Relish on water biscuits and some chicken liver paté which was Julieta's cook's speciality and which we scooped onto melba toast in thick slabs. Eustace sat at the pianola and pumped with his feet and *Oh My Darling Clementine* went round and round while Lady Grace skulked in Julieta's bedroom and the old crone laughed, then smiled, then looked wistfully back into those other lives. Sybilla danced but not if we looked at her. Eustace bellowed the words and mouthed them at Sybilla so she could learn them too and she reached out her little arms and clasped Hat-Man to her chest and went to hide behind Julieta's curtains which were chintz and had lost their glaze. Then it was *Camptown Races* and Eustace's legs pumped and pumped and he sang until the sherry and the paté were finished.

All the way to the boatyard and then to the dock and then onto the water. Eustace like a balloon. He was going to pop, to break his moorings, to soar away up, soar away. His hair was in his eyes and his hands were barely controlled, flexing and fidgeting, longing to move. For the past month or two, he had banned us, worked alone – it's a surprise, for you, for my angels – and we could see from a long way off as we shuttled towards the jetty the big new red sign on her stern that read Ann of Goole and the outside paint of her and the brand new shine of her and the sweat he had poured for her doing all those things, the big job, the money, the labour, the love. Sybilla sat on the bench-seat between us, Hat-Man in her lap, while Eustace steered the old estate car dockside and Eustace kept telling her, not telling her, saying just you wait, just you wait, wanting to trip ahead of himself, wanting to spoil his own surprise by describing it all, wanting her face to light up and beam and her to squeal, maybe clap, already, now, even though we were not quite there.

He pulled up and we got out and it was as though we had changed planets. I can still remember it. I can still remember understanding at that exact moment when our feet left the old estate car and hit the jetty how much Eustace had done, how much he treasured his hopes, how much his family, this family was like chocolate buttons and cherry jam and a long suck on a hookah pipe and a lying back on the velvet cushions of ecstasy and a sun and a moon and a breakfast. I can still remember feeling the burn that Eustace had inside him on that day. He looked larger than ever. Taller, thicker, broader. The sun lay across his face, behind and above him. We walked beyond the jetty to the river. I think he wanted to hold it back even though he did not want to hold it back. The sun turned and went behind him as the river – his shrine – was behind him. He wanted to speak. He wanted to cry out. That is what I thought then and that is what I remember now. I remember him scooping her up and holding her high against the river-bright sky. I remember his love that day, it was a moon-love, a Mars-love, a love from all of Venus. He gave it to us. He was giving it to us.

CHAPTER IV

Now we slept on the river. From that day and forever. The water was our cradle, the stars were our canopy, all around us, the coots shrilling and the boats tipping and colliding and the ropes clipping their masts and a swan or a gull or ducks joking. Eustace built a stable for the rocking-horse outside in front of the wheelhouse so Sybilla's mount could stay on the deck and his brass-studded saddle would not be damaged.

I sewed. I sewed not just our life and our story but I went back to organza, to silk, to fur, to linen, to lace. I began to sew portraits and landscapes. I went to a theatre because I wanted to do more, to use the hands I had been given to make the stories that others could take away with them and relive. And I persuaded them because I too had some fire, I knew that I could sew and make something more than the sum of the parts and soon I sewed characters, people, scenarios. A whole cast of a Shakespeare play, the Malvolios and the Violas and the Aguecheeks took their place across the cabin of the top deck. Old coats and old bolts and old dresses and here and again some curtains and I worked them – sometimes out of nothing – into cloths of gold, into the backdrop of someone else's vision, into forests and clearings and jokers and maids. I sewed and when I think of it now, my fingers became a blur as they flew across expanses of this toile, that slub.

The fog of my fingers and the grunt and the hefting and the sheer will of Eustace while he came and went, beginning to build his fortune, playing with his ship, playing with its passengers and making sure he hoped, he hoped that their journey, our journey was not just plain sailing but golden, to the stars and back joyful. One night he told me that he had remembered something from his childhood. He had remembered being at school at the end of the school-day waiting for his mother and he was young, maybe just nine, maybe younger and she was coming, he knew she was, she had told him that morning she would come and he was waiting and he was waiting and he remembered the cold of the gate that he held onto while he waited for her and how he took his hand off and there were flakes of paint stuck to his lifeline and he remembered the teacher coming out and he remembered it was nearly dark by then.

Those years and Sybilla's legs took more cloth to cover and my fingers flew for her as well, while she went to her little school just near the boatyard, in a small house with a garden, and I layered and fashioned and plumped her. I made a suit for Hat-Man because I thought it would be good if we knew where Hat-Man was. Eustace asked if he could be the one to dress Hat-Man and Sybilla took the suit and held it up to her chest and she danced off with it, a spinning circle of smocking and petticoat, out of the cabin that Eustace had made plank by plank and onto the deck that he had painted inch by inch and into the stable and we could hear her footling, scraping the ground as she shunted her horse, and we did not see Hat-Man's suit again until yesterday, after the storm.

CHAPTER V

Once he had plated and re-plated her and built her and rebuilt her, once he had made every part of the deck and the boat safe and we had moved there and lived there and he had gone to his big job and begun to learn his new trade, Eustace turned his mind to the wheelhouse and the engine room because all along what he wanted, he told me, was for us not just to sit on the river but to know her. One day, he said, he would stand at the wheel and he would sail her. Moving along in the dark and knowing that we were there, Sybilla and I, moving with him, asleep, safe, with him. Not night walks but night sails. The river he said had flowed through his life even though his mother and father had left him without warning. When he was younger, still looking for them, he dropped bottles with messages, bottles upon bottles, thinking they might reach the sea and the sea might take them to his mother. He had gone to that bench and waited, he had promised the teacher, promised her that he would be fine, that he would find his mother on the bench still waiting, then bending his fingers because they were stiff, peeling the flakes of paint off because they were itchy, he walked off with his satchel in the other hand

and he knew the teacher was watching him so he went smartly and he went to the bench which was indeed one his mother and he had sat on together once – and she was not there and he did not see her again.

We had been there for two years, maybe three and Sybilla was six or seven and it was November and the air was thick with winter, and Eustace said I am almost ready, we will go for a night-sail and he said Sybilla my angel would you like to hold the wheel, one time, we can sail along the river, through the stars, listen to the city sleeping and she said could Hat-Man. And Eustace laughed, he did not mean to, he told me he did not mean to, he remembered when one of the aunts laughed at him, he was a bit older, maybe ten, laughed because he said one day he would make a fortune, laughed because he said he could not remember his mother and father, laughed because she had a soul that was drier than sticks, because she had not wanted to look after her nephew or anyone at all, certainly not.

I am sitting here on the bench in the sun by the river by the quiet cannon looking east. I am looking at my fingers as they fly through it all, as threads and tassels and tails flutter past, as we danced then along the selvage. Love larger than the rains bulged out of Eustace and his lust for being was sometimes too big, for the huge coal-barge, for the wide-mouthed river, for the city, for the pared down world of Sybilla whose skin was like gossamer, who was eggshell fragile, whose smile when it came lasted for a year.

And then at the end of that November when the days were barely distinguishable from the dark, he did it, he made the engine turn and the wheel turn, he made the lock keeper lift the gate and his burst out laughing moment was gone and she stood there, beneath the moon-and-stars clock with the light from his dials glowing under her chin and he stood over and behind her, while she held the wheel and Hat-Man held the wheel and we moved forward into the river that was part of the night, through the city that slept, beneath the stars where she belonged.

I am sitting here on the bench in the sun by the river by the quiet cannon looking east watching the wake of Ann of Goole as the old coal barge woman swan goddess behemoth swept us all into the face of that aunt who had laughed at Eustace when he was a boy, into a night-sail that preceded many, into moments with the lock-keeper when Eustace spoke to him as to an old friend, into long quiet hours when we slept and he had us with him.

PART V

EUSTACE, JULIETA, SYBILLA

CHAPTER I

Julieta told me she had met Eustace while she was having an affair with one of the aunts' husbands. Julieta was probably from Eastern Europe but she had long forgotten from which part or perhaps it was that she had never been quite sure. She believed her mother was an heiress and her father a Romanian princeling but that may not have been true at all. Her mother it seemed had had no idea what the truth was and her father had been despatched early on. At one point, they had lived in some grandeur, that she said was true. But it went, she said, death and greed took it, she said, they threw it away.

Still now Julieta wore the stoles she had exacted as prices from her lovers. Mostly ermine – and it was easy to picture her young, fur-laden, gliding like a swan through the deep waters of all those cities, waltzing on her looks, on her fine, high brow and her swooping lashes and her eyes which were as almond-shaped as her fingers were long as her form was willowy as her natural ways were still even now as lovely as a mountain stream.

She worked a little here, she said, she partied a

little there, she married now and again. By the time she was forty-three, she was living in a third-and-fourth-floor flat in a tenement that looked over this river. It was paid for by one of the lovers, given to her in an access of love she said, filled with trinkets he bought for her, the pianola, the long-case clock, the Aubusson carpet. She had one poodle and one small brown terrier. Flashes of the old childhood place came back to her, the Peacock Garden, the Crystal Room, the fireplace large enough to hold whole families, the park and the park trees and the rampart walls. She remembered the squirrels that ran the crenellations. She remembered the brazier on the roof and the secret cellar. In her tenement flat, she had two spare bedrooms and one December when the sky was inky black and she was alone, she heard a cry from the past, a call from her ancestors, she said, a long-ago bleat from the people who had worked there at the castle. Do not let this be forgotten they said, do not let more go. And overnight – while that past that they had squandered through death and greed held her, span her round, mocked her, blindfolded her, then unblindfolded her and she could not reach it and she could not hold on and rooms and memories and gardens and people just slid into oblivion – Julieta decided to abandon the notion of husbands, to grasp on to her albeit modest mooring in this world, to treasure the pianola and the aspidistra and the love of God and take in lodgers. This too could not pass, she thought, she could not let that happen if only because of the dogs.

Eustace's uncle had been Julieta's penultimate lover. She saw him a few times, she said, Eustace, as a child and once or twice as a young man. He was too small for his clothes and too big for his body, she said. His dark brown eyes were haunted. He did not smile, not then. Had she been able to stay, she said, she would have talked to him. But as it was, darling, I was only ever there on the sly.

She told me she had had over seventy-five lodgers in her life, most of them – though not all, mind you, Isabella – young men like Eustace who were on the cusp of becoming themselves. Julieta told me that Eustace told her he wanted to sleep in a high-up room with views over the water and she was able to reply that she happened to have vacant just the thing. Julieta told me that Eustace was the only one of the young men who stayed in her house who treated her as a woman. When he moved into that high room with the views, he was nineteen and an art student and the haunted look she remembered from a few years before had grown into him.

He lived in that room for three, maybe four years, she did not remember exactly, it must have been until he met you darling. What she did remember exactly was the space he filled up and the space he did not. She fell, she said, a little in love with the boy – yes, darling, I know, I know – but his presence and more notably, when he was out at college and later out teaching at the school, his absence reminded her of the morning after some ball she had attended long, long in the past. She in a red sequinned floor-length three-hooped velvet crinoline, her suitor in a primrose-yellow tailcoat with high white stock and when the ball was over, when the champagne had run out and the dancing, all she took back to her room was a broken heel on her shoe and some missing sequins. One day, she said, Eustace brought her a photograph he had found in a junk shop of her old castle and she had put it on top of the pianola and trembled for a life that had been needlessly wasted and wondered what Eustace might become.

CHAPTER II

I often went to see Julieta. The shawl she gave us from the camomile days and her childhood in the big turrets was one of our treasured possessions. Her stories were those too, treasured, harking back to a time that was both entirely different and exactly the same. People with promise and people blighted by folly. Dogs. Necklaces. People who worked for you. People you worked for. People who loved you. People you loved. She was grand, of course she was grand, you could see it in her neck. She had mischief in her past and love and sex and diamonds. And she had grief. And loss. And her family was a sham or at least she was not sure that it was not. In her tenement, which makes it sound as though it were not a gracious, high-ceilinged apartment with lovely rooms, we talked. I told her about the north coast. We discussed Eustace. We talked of Sybilla.

From Julieta, I understood why Eustace referred to the aunt who took him in as someone with a soul drier than sticks. I learnt too that he was born that way, that what he had was what God had given him, a kind of power that made him more powerful, more big, more present than anyone else and that made him at the same time more silent, more vulnerable, more unable to cry out. Yes his stupid selfish parents left him, just walked out, she said, it was a cause célèbre at the time, they disappeared from the city, from the map, abandoned their son, abandoned their lives, no trace. It was only years later, Julieta said, that someone found them, they were living at the far end of the world, not murdered or kidnapped or lost after all, just living, hiding. But that was not what formed him, she said, he was already too big for them, too giant in his soul, too bright an object for their flat-footed selves. For Eustace, said Julieta, to be young was not easy. His charisma was not just a mystery to himself – everything was too small for him, the teachers' ambitions, the teachers' knowledge, the pencils, the desks – but a mystery to those around him. Although it was not clear what talent he had exactly, it was clear that he had talent and it annoyed them, the others. No friends.

As a child, she said, and I barely knew him then, he was not like a child. Three ways round he missed out on childhood – because his parents withdrew it from him, because his aunts did not understand childhood or children or even people, because it was not within him to enjoy childhood, he was never a child, only a forcefield, only an unexploded bomb.

It was natural that we discussed Eustace and she told me about the little flat that he shared with the aunts. The aunts had not been educated, she said, deprived of going to school and that had soured them, she said, they were clever the aunts, mathematical some, inclined to books the others, but they shared a unique quality of bitterness, she said. I suppose said

Julieta that Eustace spoiled their fun. Without him, they could have indulged their shared resentment more freely. With him, they were forced to realise that there were other things, that life could also offer joy.

CHAPTER III

And just as we discussed her past and what she knew of Eustace, so we talked of Sybilla. Somehow by some means without all that much to go on from the very start, Julieta understood. She walked up the stairs that day when Sybilla was still so young, barely formed, soundless and she saw. You might have thought she would be steeped in auntness, in old ladyness, in single-womanness, weighed down and blinded and skewed in vision by no-childness. You might have thought she would bring from her lost grandeur one pointing finger that did not look ahead but harked back. She should have been too old to understand and too spoilt. Her heart should have been too blackened by the thin grasp her parents had held on the truth and the thin grasp she held on them.

Julieta was none of those things. She was a chiaroscuro of a woman, gentle and at the same time bold, flippant and at the same time profoundly humane, caustic at times, modest, generous, seeing at others. No children perhaps, not much to leave the ancestors or appease them with, but all the same, a perfect understanding of what it was like, to be young, to be out of place.

She formed a bond with Sybilla which was silent and as close and silent as her bond with Lady Grace or with the dogs that lived in her bed. She understood at once about Hat-Man, when we brought him back from the end of the river and Sybilla plonked him down on the table next to the aspidistra. Sybilla trusted that understanding from the start and when we stayed for tea, Julieta would have the cook make an extra scone with extra jam and extra double cream, very small, just for him. Their bond was a sitting on the lap bond, a fiddling with her jewels bond, a please can you tell me a story bond. Something about Julieta helped to open up something in Sybilla. Maybe it was Julieta's scent or the magic of the pianola or the books that were absolutely everywhere in piles. Sybilla moved up a school and now she was taught next door to the gracious flat and in time, I let her walk round to Julieta's at the end of the school day and I would meet her there. When I did arrive, she might be sitting on the princeling's daughter's lap and they were sharing Hat-Man. Or looking together – while Sybilla idly twisted Julieta's string of black pearls – at the photograph of the castle that Eustace had brought her and Sybilla might be quietly asking her castle questions, how many secret rooms, how many ghosts, how many underground tunnels.

Sybilla knew Julieta from the start and it was a refuge for us, for me, to come and have tea with Julieta and see the little girl so comfortable, so alight. I thought of myself with my grandmother on the north coast and wondered if my mother might have seen the same when I was with her mother, a transformation in me engendered by friendship with someone of such a different age. The magic of the old, the fairy-tales, the impossible stories about socks and Bonnie Prince Charlie. Perhaps Sybilla felt – each time she climbed into the old crone's lap – that she too was walking among turrets and princelings. Perhaps she felt that the gossamer thinness of her skin was safe against the porcelain beauty of Julieta's. Or maybe it was simpler than that, that up through Julieta's lap, out of Julieta's soul sprang love and it was a love without expectation and that was all.

CHAPTER IV

At his studio, Eustace was making the long slow transformation from slave to master. Five years in and now he was allowed to conceive ideas, not just to put them into form. The studio worked on monumental studies, town emblems, city promises, grand structural gestures that saluted great men of the past or lost men, sometimes women, sometimes beasts. Their war memorials. Their ornamentations of pillar-tops or cathedral choirs. Their sculptures.

Those were years when we treasured Eustace's day-time presence. There were not words so much as deeds. If Sybilla was not at school, it was not a school-day, he would turn her gaze on her, give his thoughts to her. Come Sybilla my darling, hold my hand. And they would walk out onto the deck and he would sit her next to him and show her. On those days, Ann of Goole became his workshop. There was a table on the deck that he had fashioned from a tree he had felled on the farm where we worked at the beginning. Clay, lumps of clay. I have an idea, Sybilla my darling, will you help me. This is what he said one radiant July's day and we had his daytime presence and it was not too hot. A bucket full of clay. He handed her some and together, they moulded it, small models at first. He lined them up like the pairs going into the Ark, only they were not in twos, they were in one long string. The models were abstract and yet they were not. They were blobs and yet they had pathos. Sybilla sat next to him on the bench he had also made from the tree he had felled to match the table. She watched him. She tilted her head to one side, then lay it on the table and watched his big fingers as they worked. The glow from the burnished yew shone on her sideways face and I saw her eyes following everything he did, every move he made with his hands. Eustace knew. He was inside himself but he knew. He was far away dreaming, I guessed, about these small abstract figures once they were made large, huge, once they took a form he was as yet concocting – and yet he was not so far away because there was something of the showman that day, in the way he put each figure once it was done onto the yew with a flourish, onto the very perilous edge of the yew looking down onto the deck as though it were the plunging sea, in the way that he allowed himself once or twice to look left and see that his angel who belonged among the stars was truly connected with his work and so with his restless soul.

He felt her watch him and he saw her watch him and he suddenly spoke out loud, shall we make Julieta a present? and Sybilla clapped, she said yes, she said Hat-Man says yes too and I watched them together, father and daughter, plotting it, they were not sure what, perhaps a Lord Grace for Lady Grace, perhaps a telescope so she could look back into the past and see her lost castle. They discussed it or at least Eustace asked Sybilla what she thought, what would be best.

He wanted not just to love her, he wanted to know her. He wanted not just to make a stable for her horse or an emblem for their old friend, he wanted to know her, know his daughter, see her from inside, be able to understand the world as she understood it, to laugh when she laughed, to point towards the same things at the same time and say 'Look' and then say 'Snap'. I see them now again at that table while the blobs that bore not just his hand prints but hers lined up along the edge of that surface and peering over and Eustace with his piece of clay is trying to tease her out. I see her face looking at him but she is not looking at him, she is watching his hands and perhaps the gap between them is growing smaller but I cannot be sure. He wanted still to take out his paws from inside his paws so he could feel her, really feel her, understand how this elfin, delicate, beautiful creature, how she moved from one moment to the next, how she planned, how she dreamt, what she saw. He told me once he longed for her to grow up so that they could talk but that was not true, he did not long for her to grow up, he just longed for her. He did not want her to grow up because every moment with her – no matter how vexed with misunderstanding – was treasure to him, pure gold.

CHAPTER V

Eustace worked as he had worked on the baling and the calving and the scrubbing of fishing-boats and the plating and re-plating of Ann and now it was for the making of bronzes and the hewing of stones. The studio was an old bonded warehouse, bricks on bricks on bricks, pulleys, high windows, triumphal-arch-high spaces and there were apprentices and there were men who fired and men who poured hot bronze. It was poised on the river and this pleased him too and he told me how he was glad to have wasted all that time at art college drawing things. Yes, now, his was a larger canvas, he could stand on the top floor of the warehouse and imagine his figures lining the river, rising up in mutiny or after-deathness, waving their swords at the past, giant, megalithic.

On the deck of Ann of Goole, when he rehearsed his work, it was always to make a line of blobs that marched along, faceless and yet full of expression, formless and yet not. He had this vision, he said, and one day it would be made real. They were ghosts he said, lost souls, he said, and he did not understand in particular why they haunted his work but, he said, they do not leave me, he said, they turn and turn inside my head and I may not rest until I put them down.

Did we ever talk about it? When we were lying in our cabin overlooked by dipping fronds of velvet and sequins that mimicked the stars. When the tick of the clock in the wheelhouse moved us forward to the rhythm of those batting eyelids and the Alice-in-Wonderland smiles. When I told him I was pregnant again, surprise, good surprise, and he held me as though, if he did not, he would fall off.

Did I have a plan in my mind when I took him back to those memories of the north of the country where I had learnt about birds and heather, light and wind with my grandmother? When I spoke of home, small, crouched, old that it was but full of more stories, my mother and her clavichord, my mother and her songs that were diffused with Celtic longing, my father with his stoop and his bony knees and his passion for stacking logs as though the world at any moment might grind to a halt? That if I talked like this, Eustace might somehow dislodge from inside him the stories he had forgotten about his childhood and we could start from there, rummaging around in his coaly black sack of nothing until we found a thing or maybe two that would please his eyes?

Did he have a plan when on those evenings, winter, summer, it did not matter, he announced we would be going on a night sail and he took to the wheelhouse with the glow of the dials beneath his chin and we set forth, the talk with the lock-keeper, the clunk of the locks, the groans of Ann of Goole who wanted to rest and yet loved the open river because that was – in the bones of her – what she knew? I lie here now in the bosom of Ann and go over it all. He told me, when I told him about the new baby, when I told him and his joy made the velvet above billow and swell, that one day he too would give birth of sorts for it had come to him – while he was working on his ghosts – that some day he should cast Sybilla. He should carve her and mould her. He should rend her. He should make something, a likeness of her, a tribute to her, a gift to her, a gift.

He would cast her aboard, he said, another rocking-horse, only this would be a life-sized charger, 17 hands, carved and moulded from steel, dappled grey, an Irish Draught with a rising arched neck and a long white free-flowing tail, its thick haunches supple, able to dance as warhorses can, as they did, piaffes and levades and airs above the ground of all kinds the like of which made seasoned warriors tremble; and she would ride it, small but intent, proud as Boadicea, emboldened as we all can be by the power of the horse. Would you my darling make the saddle cloth and of course I would, of course.

Sometimes I think we were just selfish. We were proud of her and in love with her and at the same time, we did not see her. Then again I know that I am wrong to think that because I know this story is not about me and Eustace so much as it is about Eustace and Sybilla and I do not think that the answer to this story lies in anything so simple as parents who were closer to one another than they could be to their child. This story is about that man, whom I loved so much that it hurt to see him trying so hard with the clay to make his little girl let him in. This story is about that girl and how she, in a hundred thousand ways, was so unlike him and, in another hundred thousand ways, suffered in exactly the same way as he did. This story is being told by me because I watched it, every moment of it, every breath. I watched this great gas cloud of love that hovered over them, between them, yet was out of reach because she was what she was and he was so much what he was, too big for his clothes, too small for his giant soul. I remember that day as though it was today, now when I am sitting on the deck with Eustace and I have told him, with my boots almost breaking my ankles and my coat hanging off my shoulders, that she is found.

PART VI

FREDA

CHAPTER I

Freda came, Freda came, she joined us one October afternoon when the leaves were falling from the weeping poplars and Ann of Goole's deck was catching them all. She came and we were all there, Eustace, Sybilla, Hat-Man, even Julieta who did not have another shawl she said but she did have an ivory rattle with silver bells. Freda came and she was the spit of Eustace, she was a smile, she was a laugh, a laugh that was trying and failing not to come, a bursting-out-loud laugh, her face like the face of the moon-and-stars clock. Dimpled cheeks and dark hair. Julieta said she had a photograph of herself when she was born and in Freda, she saw something familiar. Not just the rattle she had brought us but a look, she said, a flavour.

Sybilla was enchanted, from the moment we came back and I laid Freda down in the same drawer we had had in the chambre de bonne. Spent hours with the baby girl showing her Hat-Man, talking to her in Hat-Man code, pooling lengths of cloth I had imported for my latest play around Freda, as though she were Ophelia among the rushes. For a moment, we thought that Hat-Man might lose his place to Freda for they danced together, cavorted onto the deck and back indoors, Sybilla holding her mascot close and firm.

Ann of Goole sighed. Ann of Goole stretched out as though the river was holding her at either end so she could take in the sun and join the smile that was Freda.

And Eustace? Of course it was easy for him to love her at first sight and for always because she was Eustace, made from the bark of him and the flesh and the branches and the leaves of him. Even at a few months old, she had his mannerisms, the turning of her head to one side, the drawing up of her hand to her mouth to hide who knows what, a stop, don't-hurt-me kind of gesture that she did not lose until the day she died. Freda gurgled. Freda was greedy. Freda soon sat up on her square fesses and squealed at Sybilla whenever Sybilla came back from school or in from on deck or up from below deck, squealed with piggy pleasure to see her new ally in this new world of hers. I was doing operas now, fingers in a different kind of blur because there was *Norma* and her priestess robes to make and there was Freda to watch and Sybilla to watch too, to make sure that this new one did not topple the existing one, to keep an eye on the delicate spider's web of feelings that laced itself across Ann of Goole, tangible and yet hard to see.

On our first night sail after Freda was born, for once I did not lie there in the cabin and allow Eustace to dream alone. I meant to go to him but first I went below to check on Sybilla, to check on Freda and the drawer was empty, Freda's tiny cabin was empty and I went into Sybilla's and there they were curled up around one another, slight, beautiful, elfin ten-year-old girl, young India rubber-ball of joy asleep within. Eustace held the wheel and looked along the silken ribbon of the river and but for the rumble of the engine, all was quiet. I stood behind him, I held onto him and together we dreamed of Viking longships and the snows of Sutherland and the lines of stone ghosts that one day would be made real.

CHAPTER II

Eustace began his sculpture of Sybilla with the horse. Naturally enough. The giant charger was no small endeavour and took its time to emerge. Eustace drew and then made a model but the horse eluded him, airs above the ground indeed while it danced just slightly out of his reach. Eustace came back to it again and again, when he was not at his studio, when he was not dandling Freda or cooking – something he now did with the gusto of a Mediterranean chef, flinging pans and garlic and pasta and snails and slivers of something lip-licking delicious, maybe fresh hake, maybe double cream and freshly ground black pepper and parsley which he grew by the bucketful among the camomile.

When it rained, he drew the beast indoors at the table where we ate or on the floor with his hips above his head on his elbows, lost in thought. Sybilla liked to get down with him, when she was not preening or dressing or tickling or feeding or walking Freda, and she too had her hips above her head, saying nothing. Eustace did not tell her, she did not know that this was to be hers, this great beast of war, that she would take her place aboard one day when it was done.

They were the best of times. I cannot hold them

any longer, give them form. I can only give them colour and texture, dark green of the velvet, deep red of the velvet, amber of the wooden floor, rum-dark of his hair, rum-gold of hers, bright white of the light that bounced up from the water – whether it rained or not – sunshine of the tomatoes and garlic, rich promise of the cream speckled with his favourite freshly ground black pepper. I found his drawings the other day, sketches of the horse, the hock in particular, the jawbone too, the arch of the neck. Drawings on drawings on drawings. He wanted to make this horse real but not real real, dream real, myth real, not unicorn myth but legend myth, Bucephalus myth. He had taken to this project not just as an artist or a draughtsman or as a sculptor but as an engineer, drawing the sinews over the bones, the tendons, tiny little splint bones and ear muscles and flexors and suspensories and it was an act of great giving, an act of deep, primeval endeavour to bring this myth into life and onto our deck. Perhaps the love that he had while he was plotting, while he was holding in his mind this future in which the horse would be done and his girl would be proud, so proud and high, so high; this future in which once the beast had been unveiled, something else would be uncovered, the mysterious breach between them, the strange gap that bound them – perhaps it poured out of him as warmth from a fire and we sailed along in that glow for the years it took him to bring the horse to life. I remember those days and they were the best of times. The bums in the air and the elbows on the ground and the mix of observing and conceiving, eyes, thoughts, minds, hands, two memories, two souls. I remember the feeling on those Sunday afternoons that Eustace gave out somehow, his trying, his willing and I believed that if he could have made that beast flesh, made it cannonade out of his imagination and onto the deck and over the deck and across the jetties and along the walkways and over and up and into the battlefields and the vast green spaces of her wanderings, stirrups, mane, sunflower-gold hair flying, he would have done all that and more.

CHAPTER III

Of course if he wanted to make a model of Sybilla herself – and I know that he did – and he wanted to keep it a surprise – and I know that he did that too – the thing became more of a dance. In the drawer below the drawer that had been a cot and the drawer below that where the sketches of the horse were stashed, I found more drawings, piles and piles of them, of Sybilla. He had separated them out from the horse drawings and it turned out they spanned much of her childhood. This I had not known. Many of them share a certain fey quality, elusive, and it took me some time to see that this was not only a reflection of how Sybilla was but it was also a reflection of how Eustace tried to draw her, without her knowing, on the sly. You might want to say that it was thus that he went wrong, not marching up to her but sidling, not declaring himself to her but waiting for her to declare herself to him – and you would be wrong because in all other respects Eustace did no such thing, he never sidled and it was only because he loved her so and was so intent on showing her, on making her understand this, feel this, that he wanted to make this surprise so many years long, so many hours deep. What took me aback that day when

I found them was that this project had been in his mind almost since we had arrived from the shed-house on the coast and landed on Ann of Goole. Studies of her face, in profile of course, silhouettes of her. Sometimes there was just a line or two and I knew Eustace well enough to know that this line, that one belonged to Sybilla. There was something about them that belonged to God and I could not – not that day when I found them, not now when I look over them again – pin down what it was. He was by his own avowal no draughtsman, no portraitist. He was not interested in microscopic detail, in the flower she might have held in her hand, in the crease she may have had in her dress. He did not specially get the shape of her eyes right or the wave of her hair. And yet somehow they were, each one, a love letter to her and a love letter to his love for her – separately and together, from God.

CHAPTER IV

And so we danced through that year and the year after and the year after that. Freda grew into the dresses I made her and the dresses that Sybilla had long since cast off. Freda graduated from a drawer, not quite to a chest of drawers or a wardrobe but to her own cot bed which Eustace made from the pieces of yew he had not needed for the table. There were night sails. There were struggles with the plans for the blobs. There were mumblings about the creation of a giant bestiary, unsung corpses lining up along a cliff face perhaps, a seaside. Could this be where the blobs would go? The idea gripped him but the plan was vague. Sundays would see him practise, for himself, for Sybilla. I see him again at the table and now while Sybilla is at his side and watches, Freda is on his lap and there are fat fingers covered in pinkish slime.

When Freda was almost five, we decided we would have a party. There had not been many over the years, though we were happy enough, but a hot September beckoned and Freda would go to school after that and Eustace was in high good spirits, he had moved up the ladder at his studio, there was a talk of a big commission, who knows, maybe the ghosts. Julieta of course was guest of honour and the lock-keeper came – for some reason, one I never understood, Eustace had given him the nickname Axe-Happy Sam – and Sam sat on top of the yew table drinking straight from the bottle. One or two of the apprentices from the studio were also there and we had a brazier on the roof of the main cabin and Eustace seared a couple of the big white fish he had caught in the river only a week or two before. Julieta's hat had a brim that was so large, it almost acted as a parasol for Freda who sat at her feet, as well as Sybilla who stood by her side. We did not have a pianola or even a recorder but we did have spoons and Eustace played them – awash inside with the lock-keeper's hooch – sitting on the large Gothic velvet armchair which I was preparing for Banquo's ghost, legs akimbo, head pointing downwards, hands and wrists and fingers working until the sum of the sound of that flying silver brought people out from their houses to stand on their balconies to listen. Even Axe-Happy Sam, who had downed two bottles and was half way through a third, was brought to silence and I could see by her shadow that Julieta was spellbound and I could feel by the way they clasped my hands that Freda and Sybilla did not want him to stop.

And later, once the sun had gone down, climbing onto the roof as we all did and we danced round the brazier with the flames low but red and somewhere across the water I saw a cat stalking a coot and in the back of my mind, I hoped the coot would be seen off once and for all but in the front of my mind it was nothing but a blur of spoons and smoke and thank the water gods for everything and I looked down through the glass in the roof and saw Sybilla and Freda, the

one on the lap of the other and a small space in front
of them and there were three plates and on top of each
an almond biscuit which had been brought by Julieta,
made by her cook, enclosed in a tin decorated with
wooden grenadiers.

CHAPTER V

Freda went to school and Eustace went to the studio and Sybilla went to school and I stayed on Ann of Goole making more Malvolios and by now some Brunnhildes. Sybilla came back from school one day at lunchtime, she had made Julieta bring her, and she was dreadfully pale and shaking and I asked her, Sybilla my darling what is the matter and Julieta shook her head because she had obviously tried already. What is the matter my darling and Sybilla did not weep and she did not speak either but she wandered up and down the deck and she was fraught with something she could not put into words. Freda came back from school in the company of her friend Betsy and Betsy's mother and I had to ask them to leave at once because whatever it was with Sybilla, we had to find it out and we could not while there were Betsies and their mothers about. Julieta said she would leave and as she left along the jetty, I noticed vaguely, though not properly, that she limped these days, that one shoulder was lower than the other, and I should have jumped into the old estate car to take her but it was Sybilla, she was our treasure, for thirteen years now our angel, Eustace's angel, and

I had to help her because we knew, I knew how deeply she felt things when she suffered.

I suppose if I were to be honest with myself, I would have said that I was not surprised there had to come a reckoning. For weeks and perhaps months now, Sybilla had been that tiny bit more strained than we were used to. I wondered if Freda – her going to school or her presence in the first place or her jovial bouncy pigginess or something she simply said – had been at the root of this change. But then again I did not admit the change, not to begin with, not really. Eustace was wrapped up in his work, studio this, studio that, coming home late, spending hours scraping the clay out of the rifts in his skin. He was the same wonderful enormous-hearted Eustace but I did not trouble him with something I was not prepared to face myself, I did not. Billows of velvet and hardly any night-sails and there was life, threading past us like the river.

That night however I said to him, she is strange Eustace, she is unhappy Eustace, she will not tell us – and he went straight away from the cooker where he was tossing pans and peppercorns and I saw him down on his knees next to her, chocolate hair in his eyes, always in his eyes, taking her hands in his, what is it my darling, what is it? She did not say, I saw that much, she pulled her hands back. The waves were closing over her. And while we noticed it and while it opened up a small dark hole in the loveliness of those days, we did not remember it.

The next day there was more studio and there were more Valkyries and there was walking and fetching and scrubbing and living to do and maybe we thought she was at that age, that time when girls become agitated and withdrawn and maybe we did not think enough.

After a few weeks and it was the same, I spoke to Julieta who was thinner I thought, paler and she said why do you not all go for a time back to the cottage by the sea where you all were at the beginning? I kissed Julieta because sometimes her grand ways and her hanging onto cooks and memories of park trees were shot through with just the right kind of understanding and we all climbed into the estate car that was by now closer to its component parts than it was to viable transport machine and clunked our way back down the roads that became greener and bumpier the closer we got to the sea. Sybilla did not seem to be moved when we pulled up through the field next to the cottage, by the flagstones with the buttercups and the daisies poking through. I knew she remembered this place just as Julieta knew, because sometimes she described it to Hat-Man when she thought we were not listening, when she bowed down and held him up and spoke straight into his eyes.

Sybilla stepped out of the back of the car. I suddenly saw her as a young beauty. I suddenly saw the woman she would become with that strange hypnotic distance. I suddenly knew what it was, how could I have been so stupid, how could I have been so blind? There was no longer a space in front of her. Hat-Man had gone.

PART VII

JULIETA DIED

CHAPTER I

And then there was another thing. Straight after. It was the most surprising thing. It was the worst thing. Outside of our own lives, we had had no-one but her and suddenly the cook sent a message via the lock-keeper via a carrier pigeon and maybe via the wind itself and the message said Julieta is ill and I think she is very ill and I think you should come. I did not believe the message, not the thrust of it, not the urgency of it, not that we should come. Eustace, when I told him, did not believe it. We sat on the deck in a heap after the journey and together did not believe it. All the deaths. All the people we had not known at the end. All the people we had let down, as we saw it, my grandmother, his parents, his cold misery of an aunt. The aunts. We sat on the deck and did not think about Sybilla or Freda or anyone else except our own disappointments to ourselves.

We were selfish. That is what I see now, now that she has been found and I am thinking.

When the carrier pigeon came with the wind and a note that said you must come now, we had just returned via a breakdown truck from the farmhouse at the far end of the river. The time there had been golden, for all that we understood that Hat-Man had left us. Sybilla had been brave and Freda had held her hand, hanging from her older sister like a stuffed bear, like the smallest elephant. We had fossicked in the shoreline for old things, some very old. We had counted the daisies and noticed their spread among the flagstones. We had eaten fish and cockles and samphire tossed in the same pan that had been Eustace's mainstay during the farming years. We had walked, in a line like sheep, along the coastal path. We had cupped our hands over our eyes and looked into the horizon to spot the ships. We had picnicked at the lighthouse. We had said hello to the farmer with the cows and the other with the hayfields. We had basked.

We came back and we were brown. We came back and we threw ourselves into the embrace once again of Ann and it was good and better and smelt of all the things we remembered. Eustace said as the pigeon cast its w-shaped shadow over our heads, you go. He said you go, I will stay here. I waited. I did not go at once. I was selfish and he was selfish and we were happy and could not bear to be unhappy again.

He said I will take them for a night sail and at last I said I will go.

And I went. I walked against the river and for some reason I missed the bridge and stayed on the wrong side for too long and it took me almost double the time. When I found her, she was half-conscious, the cook by her side and the memories of the lost castle and the camomile lawn and the did-they-exist-or-not Romanian princelings. I held her hand. She was cold. She was yellowing from the inside. She asked for

Eustace – or at least, I think she did. She asked for Sybilla – or at least, I think she did, over and over. She asked for me – but maybe she did not. Her feathers and her stoles and her lovers hovered above me and I held her hand. I wanted to tell her. I wanted to say that Eustace should have been there, wanted to be there, could not be there. I wanted to reach back into her past and make it better for her, so she did not have to hide in a tenement, albeit gracious, albeit furnished with the gifts of a lover who had loved her good and true. I wanted to kiss the cook and hug the cook for being so brave and kind for her. I wanted her not to die. Because I was selfish. Because her dying would not be so much about the past as it would be about the future, about the deaths to come, about the possibility and likelihood of more sobs that would be deeper and more agonised than these. Because this had come out of a bright blue sky and the gods had not warned us. Because I loved Eustace with all my heart and thought that this could not be, this could not be.

I held her hand and thought of everything. She had framed our beginnings. She had filled his coaly black sack of nothing with her understanding. She had brought us a shawl infused with the sweet scents of her past. She had invited Sybilla onto her knee – tiny fingers wandering in and out of her strings of black pearls – and been patient while unheralded questions or silence were thrown at her. She had introduced us to Gentleman's Relish. She had introduced us to her side of the river. She had travelled the long road up the narrow stairs and brought me langues de chat biscuits, just when I thought I would not be able to survive my early motherhood, and she had folded her hands at the end of the bed and shared something with me which at the time I could not measure.

Pictures lined up in columns along the shelf behind her bed and when I was not counting the scattered hairs on her head and wondering what last memories they sheltered, I squinted into the eyes of strangers, stiff, dark-skinned, fuzzy, uniformed. Many were men and I wondered which were the princelings. The women, all of them, could have been Julieta but in earlier form, as swan-like.

In front of me and in front of Mrs Cowan who had cooked for her since the early days, in front of the memories of all of us, in front of the aspidistra and the mouldy old pianola and jars upon jars of old-fashioned condiments and the shawls she had given us and the wisdom and the jangly silver rattle, and at last in front of Eustace who had believed it finally and who had come finally having asked the lock-keeper to mind the ship and our unit while a chapter, a barely sung chapter, a woman, a friend, a person who knew most things of us, just died, just fucking well left us and died.

I am writing this now, now that our daughter, our special wonderful, strange daughter has been found. I am re-reading this now, now that she has been found. Eustace took the aspidistra and Lady Grace and me. We wheeled them along the river and there was a blur. And we walked into the blur. And we walked into the blur.

CHAPTER II

We did not wake up. Not for ages.

We did not tell Sybilla. Not for ages.

It was a mistake.

It was my mistake but above all it was Eustace's mistake – above all, above all.

It was my mistake because I am the mother, because I should be the wise one, because I am the one who holds my children closer to my chest, because a mother dies on the graves of her children, because that is the curse and the blessing of mothers.

It was Eustace's mistake because he did not see, could not see how fine and grand and brave a person he was, how fine and grand and brave a father he was to Sybilla.

We sustained a lie.

We lied to Sybilla.

By pretending it was all fine.

By pretending, hoping that she would not be touched by this.

We lied to Sybilla.

I am sitting here now and she has gone and I am bitter, with myself, because I was not honest. And I am bitter not with Eustace exactly but for him and I do not know how to say that otherwise.

Julieta died and he should have known not to bring the aspidistra back to Ann before we had explained to Sybilla. We should not have brought Lady Grace, even though she was only briefly on the boat before running away into the wilderness of the boatyards. We should have taken Sybilla with us to her flat when Mrs Cowan called in despair because in doing that, we would have shown her how much we knew she felt. Instead I sat with Julieta as she whispered into the next life and I turned round into Eustace, leant back into Eustace, let tears fall onto the crewel work bedspread she had managed to keep back from the castle, thought only of myself and us and how we had not known that she was one of the threads that wove through our cloth or at least that when that thread was withdrawn, we too would unravel. The cook made us tea and half way through, she could not continue so we put the kettle back on the stove and made the cook tea, strong tea, and she sat with her hair poking out of her cap and all you could see was the top of her head as though she wanted to fold herself in two, as though she would never look up again into the eyes of another, as though grief and shock were doubling her up inside of herself. The cook stood up again and raised her head gingerly, like her neck had almost snapped, and we could see she could not see for grief, even though we too could not see, and she handed us the cat and the plant because she wanted us to leave and she wanted us to spare her the living things, not the pianola. As we drifted through our shock along the embankment, I found myself accompanied by Julieta. There was a frisson and a stole-wrapped goddess, with the sense and sageness that good women can have and fairy-tales, took me by the elbow and told me old secrets. While she held me, I let myself lean on Eustace and the cat rested in the crook of his elbow and the river walked beside us. Men had come and taken Julieta away while we waited but they did not take everything, because by then her everything had become part of ours.

And for a week or maybe a month, for an hour or maybe ten days, I do not know how long, we were too cowardly and too stupid to tell Sybilla.

CHAPTER III

That night and for several, we slept like death. Like we had died. Not this elegant barely knowable woman who had touched our lives but us. But we. Eustace smothered me, enfolded and swamped me and his sleep was nothing and everything. Drapes draped over us, sequins shone. Ann of Goole, a wise woman herself, held us.

On the morning when we finally woke up, we had forgotten all the things – selfish – and I went to take Sybilla to school and when Eustace went down, she was on the floor of her cabin cradling the aspidistra – in front of her, in the space where Hat-Man had been.

'Why is it here? Why is it here?'

Big round blobs of sadness and they had fingers that were pointing at Eustace, at me, at our lie.

'Why is it here?'

And for too long, a life-time, there came no answer.

Did I ever mention that music was another comfort? Aside from the work on the spools and costumes, aside from the magic of Eustace's life in clay? Aside from Ann of Goole? Did I ever mention that when we drove in the estate-car which was always nearly breaking, we had a wind-up gramophone on the back seat – wedged between Sybilla, Freda and Hat-Man while he still existed? Did I ever tell you that our journeys over the bumpy tracks were accompanied by Jessye Norman singing the *Four Last Songs* or Maria Callas or Kathleen Ferrier singing almost anything? Did I tell you already that Eustace had a fine baritone and that he harmonised to Jessye or Nina or Clarence Frogman Henry and that he brought to that the same panache he brought to Spaghetti a la Vongole?

When Sybilla found us out, we did not, as we should have, I see it now, wrap her inside of us and hold her inside of us but we put on Elizabeth Leonskaja playing Chopin and then Marta Argerich also playing Chopin. There was the noise of shame and the noise of the silence that followed her question. Both had to be replaced.

The aspidistra needed water and Sybilla needed us. And I stood and Eustace stood and Sybilla sat on the floor, the empty space now filled by a willowy pot plant, and the truth was stuttered out against plangent notes of nocturnes being drawn from a piano in water. Eustace bent down to pick Sybilla up, to lift her high as he liked to do, to make it better through touch. She was too big for that now, slight though she was, and he could not make a clean sweep and she leaned away, just a bit, just enough to make it clear, how much she understood what we had done, the awful mistake.

He turned. I could feel how much it hurt him, this truth that Sybilla had pointed out. He could not make it better, not now, not like that. Freda was waiting for him, it was her turn, to go to school, to be swept up high, to hold onto her father's hair while he bounced her along the street and into the playground and she boinged up and down on her shoes, her arm stretched towards him, impatient. Did he know already that Sybilla would leave us? Did we know? Did we think that by denying her her grief, we were trying to postpone something? Postpone some breach in the happiness we had shared, up until only moments ago? Did we see into the future, did he see into the future then and understand how frail were those threads of our existence, how close to rupture? The only thing that kept us safe was an old coal-barge and a man whose heart was bigger than his body. Was that enough? Was that enough?

I do not know. I wish. If I could undo anything, it would be the nocturne.

CHAPTER IV

Julieta had left some money and two small letters. One was written on paper impressed with a simple coronet, maybe Romanian. An elderly lawyer with a pale yellow scarf and a sniff came when we were there and told us about the money. It was simple, he said, sniff. There was little and it would go to Mrs Cowan, along with the chambre de bonne. The tenement flat, it turned out, did not belong to her but to the lover who had loved her. No-one wanted the pianola or the rest, we agreed, and the lawyer said sniff he would organise a sale.

The second was in a plain envelope and we did not open it because it was addressed to Sybilla. That fact alone made me start – now she had her own life, our daughter who was fifteen, she had letters written to her, after-death letters, and if I had not already understood it, Julieta was telling me that Sybilla was. The envelope said in the beautiful copperplate handwriting of Julieta's generation To Miss Sybilla Coldwinter. I saw Eustace hold it up to the light. I saw him smell it and secrets lurked within. They smelt of the song of the river. They smelt of glittering dances and primrose coloured tailcoats. There was a hair caught in the glue of the envelope and I watched him ease it out because that was one thing too many.

In the church, it was a week or two later and we sat in a straggled line. There were men we did not know, several, sitting apart. Eustace had never seen them before he said, they were unfamiliar. There were also young people, troops of them, bees with hats and scarfs and buzzing, and we understood that you cannot ever understand, that a death reveals not a life but its mystery. A hymn was pronounced and Sybilla and Freda stood next to us and Sybilla clutched the envelope which she had not opened, I was sure, and in her other hand was Freda's. After singing, there was silence. There were words from a priest Julieta must have known because he did not sound too wrong and there were words from Eustace which I could not hear. We walked back to the boatyard, along the river for some last time along that route and the ghost of Lady Grace, who still had not been found, haunted our journey. Behind us, Sybilla.

CHAPTER V

There was the lie. There was the rotten selfish delay in telling Sybilla that her friend – and that is what we had failed to understand, that Julieta was her friend – had died. There was the bringing of the aspidistra before we had let Sybilla know. There was the disappearance of Hat-Man which was nobody's fault but that did not mean it did not count. There was Lady Grace, first there, then gone. There was the letter.

There was a visit from the school, from a teacher called Mrs Wilson who was contemptible, I knew it, by the way she walked onto the boat and, with her arms folded, drew her breasts up under her chin. I watched her eyes as they skirted over the deck, over the maquettes of the blobs, over the yew table. As they came inside and saw the velvet and saw the sequins and all the pans. This was not like school, those eyes proclaimed and I was afraid inside for what Mrs Wilson was about to say.

Eustace was not there. He had plunged himself into the workshop, busy, busier. Freda was at school, bumbling her way through her own sunshine. I had been at my sewing machine and there was the echo of Cecilia Bartoli ringing round the cabin and there was a plate, I could see it, that I had not washed.

'Your daughter has not been to school since March.'

Now it was nearly May. Now it was ducks and drakes, it was bulbs and blossom, it was sweet evenings leading to night sails. I did not know whether to apologise to Mrs Wilson or to remonstrate with her. Judgment poured from her like smoke. Her breasts climbed higher and higher. When I think about that meeting, I know I was wrong, she was kind, she had come to help. When I look back, I see that I should have been more open to her, not so leave-me-alone. Then, all I felt was a horrible surge of horribleness, like something had come towards me that had been coming towards me for some time and the only reason I had not seen it close in was because I had been keeping my eyes firmly shut. Crisp, monosyllabic, sulky, I answered Mrs Wilson in an oh-really kind of way, in a we'll see about that kind of way, in a do you mind never ever again dropping in without warning kind of way and I walked beside her to the jetty gate, wishing it had been Eustace, not me.

Sybilla came back – and now I was not sure from where – and Eustace came back and he brought Freda with him and we ate Veal a la Milanese because Eustace had been to the market and the sun went down through the branches of the oak tree whose roots had been here as long as the city. She had read the letter, I knew she had, because I had seen small tufts of Conqueror paper on the floor of her bedroom and I knew they came from the envelope. Was she different? Was there something about her, now that she had read the letter, now that I knew she was not going to school but where? Would she tell him, tell him anything? Would she let Eustace explain or at least try to – because this is their story, not mine? Would she ever climb onto his back again and sit up there like a maharani?

Outside, the coots. Outside somewhere, Lady Grace. Outside, shivering in a green tomb, Julieta. If she was here now, she would know, what to do and say, who should talk and who should stand back and cook, she would know.

PART VIII

THE FARMER'S YEAR

CHAPTER I

Looking back, I see this story as having the shape of the farmer's year. It starts in spring but perhaps the trigger for the telling is the end of the harvest, when the crops have been beaten into flattened whorls by wind and rains we had imagined would never come.

The farmer's year – the time we had with Sybilla, the time the lion kept guard over his cub – was one peppered with rainstorms, with hailstorms, with heatwaves and rainbows. Eustace worked on his model of Sybilla, on first of all the horse for Sybilla and once he took me to the workshop and there it was, growing out of his imagination and onto a plinth that was the size of giants. It was thrilling, the hind legs, the haunches, the trunk. Soon would come the withers, the base of the neck, the forelegs. I had made the tail from threads I had pulled from magic carpets until thick kinked lengths of silver could flow behind, ready to sweep the battlefield beneath its into-the-fray levades.

Eustace was wrapped up in his work and when I told him of Mrs Wilson and what she had said, I saw that it took time for the words to reach him. His blobs were no longer about to stride the river. His vision had changed, they would take their place on a steep cliff, lined up on the brow of a coastal precipice, staked there as mementoes to a past war, a past catastrophe, ghosts of lives that should not have been lost. I do not know where his story came from nor could Eustace explain it but it had a hold of him now, a grip and the blobs of clay along the edge of the table had become not men and women but a bestiary as he called it. Nights and days and this story was becoming one less of lost individuals, more of a lost tribe, unsung sacrificial victims, men and women represented not in human form but in animal, defending their boundaries and yet at the same time looking through them, men and women dead and yet coming to life, men and women armed and yet defenceless except for the sea below, except for the breaches in the land mass. Why war? But he could not say. Why so many? And he could not answer that either. Why by the sea? And maybe that was the easiest to answer, because water flowed through him, because all rivers lead to the sea and the river we lived upon held him. It had taken him gradually, a germ of it, years ago when he played with clay under Sybilla's childish gaze and now the stories were more than real to him, so real he was seeing them with the eyes of strangers. You would walk up to the cliff face and look up, high above, and see cows and horses. You would know, without having to ask yourself or anyone else, what they meant. This would be a vast project, a mammoth undertaking for any man and I wondered if every figure was a ghost that had peopled his early past.

'Let me talk to her,'

he said when finally the words landed.

'I will talk to her.'

We had chosen to come back from the workshop by the river, past Nelson's house, past the stone steps that lead to the shoreline, past rings in the river wall and ladders in the river wall that seem to go to nowhere and I had my arm in his and the water shone. Eustace gathered pace as the words took their place in his head. He walked faster, walked heavier and now the rings in the wall were no longer a feature but a blur and I sat down at the bench by the cannon and let him go ahead.

'Sybilla!'

I heard him bellow it, in his big way, in his life-large way. As he approached Ann of Goole.

'Sybilla.'

'My angel. Sybilla, my angel.'

I lost him, I lost the echo of his heavy steps, I lost sight of his profile as he rounded the corner, onto the jetty. I lost the sense of whether he kept his booming call in the major or the minor, whether he kept the purpose in his step light. I wanted it to be him that talked to her because he wanted it to be him, because his was the treaty that was more fragile, because the older Freda grew and the easier it was between Eustace and Freda, the more it mattered to him that he achieve the same with Sybilla. For myself, for me and Sybilla, it was different. She would always love me and always keep me at arms' length and that had been set out from the start. I knew that this would not necessarily change until she came to need me. I did not want that moment to arrive because it would have to be real need, like I have no water and am dying of thirst need, like I am hanging onto a razor's edge and my fingers are slipping need. I would always love her. I would always lay out cloaks of gold on the ground for her to walk on, my dreams. I would always make the saddlecloth for her rocking-horse not just with red felt and brass but with all the love and all the detail and that extra thing you have to dig out of yourself to make something not just good but previously unimagined. The mistakes that I collaborated in, the not telling her about Julieta's death, the accidental trampling of Hat-Man when he was alive and with us and our fourth man, the losing of Lady Grace, the playing of No.1 Op.9 in B flat minor when instead she should have been told, she should have been told – all these I knew, all these I held to myself like wounds. I think of that day and I think of all the days. I think of all the mistakes. I think of Mrs Wilson and her rising bosom, I think of the scraping screech of Lady Grace as she bolted from the boat and hurtled along the jetty and away from the water. I line them up and knock them down. First one goes and then they all go, flip, flip, flip, flip.

Finally Eustace emerged from the boat, from the jetty and when he came into view, I blinked towards him, trying to make out the what and the how. The mammoth and the sprite, I thought I could see them both silhouetted. I thought I could see hands that were reaching towards one another, bodies that were leaning into one another. I thought I could see Sybilla tripping along with her father as a girl might, smaller hand in large hand, smaller face looking up. I imagined the words that Eustace was saying, how he had had to swish them round in his head all the way there to the boat and let them form as he was forming his beasts, lightly and yet gravely, lightly and with all the thought, all the love. I imagined the feeling he had of his paws wanting to come out from inside his paws, I imagined his tiptoes as he tiptoed. Freda was sitting on his shoulders, way up high. That was good, I thought, a good sign. Shadows from the leaves of the poplars that lined the east side of the water dappled them. They walked round the basin once. They walked round the basin twice. I could hear Freda from the far side when she squealed with delight. Other than that, I could only guess.

Where have you been, my angel, if not at school? What did Julieta's letter say? Was it a comfort? Was it a secret, special thing that you can share? When will I know you, Sybilla? When will you let me love you?

CHAPTER II

May gave way to June. Iridescent luminescent growth segued into the stately emerald of summer. The oak tree that watched us was splendid as a tall ship. Night sails were not really night sails for the days were long and we chased the dusk only as we returned to the mooring.

My latest project was *The Rite of Spring*. It was to be filmed, outside, in the semblance of a stubble field with a cast of hundreds. Rite of Spring or more like pageant of Rite of Spring. It was to be in black and white, not the filming but the vision, the costumes like woodcuts, Nash perhaps, Ravilious, Claire Leighton. It was dance, not ballet, but it was more heaven than earth, an extravagant bonanza of monochrome versus one single stain of red that would pool in and onto the set and out of the set and into the stalls. The project was being driven by a woman, she was like a clockmaker, meticulous, slow as time. This was the project of her lifetime and I saw it would probably become the project of mine. No shortcuts. No dropped stitches. Every costume a monument, every costume the same, black and white, every one slightly different. She wanted this to be a pageant of womankind, a testament to the way in which womankind is both perceived and perceives itself. She wanted every costume to be so good that the body it enclosed became almost secondary. That she said was the point. The vision haunted me. I could see its brilliance and that is why it haunted me. I stitched and imagined and stitched and I dreamt of sacrifice.

Eustace beside me was consumed by beasts, by models of beasts, by a cliff-edge and how he could make this wall of white appear to advance towards its viewers, even though the last time the cliff had moved had been an act of tectonic shift. He was, too, consumed by the horse, by perfecting it until – he said, until – the horse was malleable, the horse had torque, the horse was so poised in every muscle that you would not believe it was not real, you would believe instead that beneath the veneer of bronze, there was the skeleton of a former charger, still snorting, fresh from the battlefield, flecked with sweat and hand-to-hand, man-to-man combat. Sometimes at night Eustace spoke of it. In his sleep and there was a Stand still or there was a Steady now and I wondered if he worked at the workshop with a live model or whether the model and the idea had taken such real form in his head that he believed when he said stand still, steady now he was not addressing himself and his own approach but he was addressing it, the real creature he was in the process of creating.

After their walk, with Freda brimming on his shoulders once, twice round the basin, Eustace said he did not think we should press the matter with Sybilla, now she was going to school again, now it was behind us. He would finish her horse soon, he said. Soon. And then he would begin on her and he could give her to her.

For once, I ignored Eustace and I visited Mrs Wilson in her study with the smell of unopened windows. I was not sure what I was going to say when I walked in – perhaps apologise for the way I had been with her when I escorted her back along the jetty, perhaps throw myself on her mercy and ask for advice, perhaps tell her the story I have told you so far – but in the event, it was not up to me. She was a headmistress and in headmistress fashion, she brooked no nonsense. Sybilla, she said, was a curious child. Our school, she said, has never yet failed. Sybilla, she said, will emerge a young lady. Of that, Mrs Coldwinter, I can assure you.

That June, they took to walking every evening, the three of them, when Eustace was not up to his elbows in clay or half-live dreams, and I sat in a sea of black and white with Jaqueline du Pré and Glenn Gould for company, with Aretha and Kris and Bill, and Ann tilted in the early summer breeze, side to side.

We were sowing then, tilling and sowing.

CHAPTER III

In the middle of the night, midsummer it might have been, midsummer it was. We had done what we did every midsummer's night and ridden the river until the final point of darkness. We had done what we did every midsummer and allowed Sybilla and Freda to stay up throughout, to watch the sun go as far as it can then turn back, to take turns at holding the wheel, to pull on the horn and play captain while the moon-and-stars clock smiled on. Ann of Goole rose up underneath us like a horse preparing to jump. We had a picnic. We had the wind-up gramophone on the deck and with the wheelhouse windows open, the river night blew Vicky Leandros and Victoria de los Angeles and the great Caruso through our hair.

Every time we went almost as far as the sea and before we reached it, we would turn, slowly as she went, slowly. The river flowed to the west and we sailed into the setting of the sun, into the turn of the year. We turned with the year. Ann turned with the year.

Since Julieta's death and Mrs Wilson's visit, Sybilla had been more difficult to read. She was present, it is true, she went to school, it is true. They went for their walks round the basin when Eustace was there and not throwing leaves and shells and legumes round and about in a hot pan or working at the studio, hours on hours. Eustace had not told Sybilla about the horse but that day, midsummer's day, he had asked her if she would like to visit the workshop. It would be her first time.

I was making the picnic, placing pieces of bakelite in size order, cutting off crusts, lashings of butter. Freda was stacking sticks on deck, one on top of another until the whole lot fell down, then again one on top of another. Sybilla had been in her chair – we all had our own chairs and hers was the blue. She had developed a habit of sitting still, in silence, with her hands one on the other, upturned. Since Hat-Man had gone, her folded hands took up the space he had left behind. I think she missed him. I think she was thinking about how to fill the space. I think she was waiting, that something might happen, that something might change. It was hard to ask her because it was hard not to say something that would be received with a bruised look or worse would disappear into her silence like a penny being dropped into a deep, deep well. Of course we were used to her but when Freda came into the room, it was so different and we realised without ever, ever saying that what we were used to was difficult, hard to understand, to navigate. I know that Eustace loved her the more she was hard to love but that did not mean she was not hard to love. Eustace turned his eyes to the blue chair and said will you come with me today, my angel, before we go on our midsummer sail, I have something I would like to show you, I think it is time and she half-closed her eyes and she did not move her folded hands and she said again, as she had before,

'You should have told me.'

It was the one time. She could not have known that he was going to show her this great magnificent structure that he was making just for her. She could not have known that by rejecting him at that moment, she was going to the very heart of what would not work between them. There was always mistiming between them, always. In many ways, that is the tragedy, was the tragedy of their story. It was the one time and she could not have known.

Eustace was angry. He had never been angry before. He had never been angry with me or with Sybilla or with anyone in my presence. He did not need to be angry. He had such natural force, of presence, of bulk, of boom and gusto that he did not need to be. No one wanted to disappoint him. His role – when he demanded it, which he rarely did – was to be pleased. To be charmed. To be thrilled. His was a countenance of tip-of-the-tongue pleasure, of waiting, expecting to be delighted. Eustace did not explode except with affection, with spontaneous bursts of Clarence Frogman Henry, with flourishes of cooking, flashes of ignited brandy. If he threw up his arms, it was in laughter. If he furrowed his brow, it was because the sun stared at him.

It was the one time I ever saw him angry and although it was little enough – a reddening, a tightening, a turning, a banging of the boat gate – it was anger and we all knew it and Sybilla knew it and even Freda squatting on her buttocks starboard-ho, even she for a moment dropped her grin.

Something about that evening, about the expectation, about the promise of the glittering sky over the water and the champagne we allowed ourselves. The picnic and the journey through the old wharfs, past the bonded warehouses with names like Jamaica and Odessa, shadows from steeples across our bows, shadows from bridges, whispered drops of conversations that sailed past us or traipsed over us, the presence of a gull or several behind us, the opening out of the river, the gradual brilliant tumble of dusk, the slowly turning, slowly as she goes. Anger could not survive this evening and Eustace held onto the wheel with the power and certainty of a man who believes he has been forgiven. His girls, so it seemed, clung to him. He held the wheel with just one hand. He laughed in the face of time and the clock, not to mock but to rejoice.

But in the middle of the night, when we had been asleep for maybe just a couple of hours and it was sleep as deep as though we were now made of the heavy velvet, there was a bang. Bolt upright. Eustace. Hair swept out of his face. Took the sheet with him, holding it round himself, seeking out the source of the bang which we both knew without thinking had something to do with Sybilla, had something to do with earlier in the day and her rejection of his offer and the anger he had given only a glimpse of. I lay and waited. Pulled the blankets up to me. Peered through the curtain at the already starting day. There was nothing to hear, no raised voices, no more bangs, just the sound of my own waiting, the lapping of the river. Eustace was downstairs, in her cabin and I pictured all the hundred ways they might be talking and the hundred things they might be saying. I pictured the bang and what it was, was it made of suitcase, was it made of leaving, was it made of secrets or were they not secrets but protests, statements? I pictured Eustace on his knees or perhaps he was at the end of her bed or was he standing up, casting a middle-of-the-night shadow over her and it was just about seeing that shadow as it was meant to be, not a blocking out of the light but a shading from the burning rays of the sun. I sniffed, was it lavender I could smell, was it oil on troubled waters, was it frankincense, the scent of offering?

When he came back with the sheet and pulled it over again and it was nearly daylight, he told me that he loved her with all his heart, that his love was something he had never expected, that he hoped to God that the giant horse with its mythic kinked silver tail would go some way to showing her just how much, that he could not wait to sculpt her, to place her in the saddle we had made together because then she would know, then she would see. He told me that he loved her with all his heart not just because she was part of me and of us but because of her, because he had never known anybody like her – child or woman – who was so deeply self-contained, so demanding of what life should give, so feeling. He knew it, he knew it. And one day he hoped she would find out, feel just that, feel that he really did know, that he really did love her for her.

Perhaps we were just trying to keep the pests and the weeds at bay then. Now I am not so sure.

CHAPTER IV

Into that radiant summer-kissed July came a friend. A friend of Sybilla's. Her name was Jennifer. Or was it Jemima? She sauntered in one day onto the boat with all the braggadocio of a chorus girl in *Carmen*. She was a year or maybe two older than Sybilla. Big wide eyes. Thick dark hair. Sexy. They had met each other at school, in different years of course but across the playground or the library or the art-room. Jemima, or was it Jennifer, told us:

'It was love at first sight, Mrs Coldwinter, Mister Coldwinter. I knew we'd be friends, I just knew it.'

She had a way of firing statements at you like arrows. She had a way of setting you on the back foot from the moment the arrow left the bow. She had a way of walking into your space like it was she and not you who belonged there. She was smart, smart as a whip. There was no magic in her, just want, just chanciness.

Eustace did not notice, not even at the very beginning. He did not seem to mind one day when he was cooking scallops, she had just dropped by, and she shoved her hand into the pan and scooped out two and put them steaming into her mouth. He did not seem to think it was strange that this unit, our carefully tended, precious unit had suddenly been disrupted by a young girl with no magic. All he could see, I suppose and we discussed it often later, was that Sybilla had a friend, that Sybilla was coming to life. Jennifer seemed to give Sybilla courage. Jennifer, or was it Jemima, the girl at any rate seemed to be achieving something that we and especially Eustace could not. Now we did not have to watch Sybilla sit in the blue chair and contemplate the space where her hands could fold. Silence and the vortex of it and the eggshells we danced on – they all just left, like a flock of swallows in September. Freda – I cannot quite put my finger on how it was different for Freda but it was and we all felt that something lifted, that a weight on our shoulders we had not known was there had lessened.

Sybilla when she was happy, when she smiled, when she had found her courage, was the moon-and-stars clock and Julieta in her ball-gown with her ermine stole and her pearl tiara and the camomile lawn with the shadow of the castle bleeding over it and Ann of Goole in full sail. She was no longer small, birdlike perhaps but the beauty we had glimpsed once, twice, a few times over the years was now all hers. She was an adult and at the same time, she was at last a child. The girl would come over most days to the boat and the sound of girls, not women, girls – sparrows arguing, bickering, chuntering in the honeysuckle – drifted upstairs onto the main deck. Sybilla began to show an interest in things, in books, in words, in the layers of light on the water, in the costumes that flew in a blur out from under my fingers. She stopped sitting in her chair, no you have it Freda, it's yours any time and she watched Eustace when he cooked and asked him about the spices. Mrs Wilson did not appear but a letter from her did and all we could read, between our tears, was the word transformation.

Sybilla when she was happy did indeed transform, not just herself, not just intransitively. Eustace seemed to grow, his hair to be more wild, his body to be larger but only in expansiveness, in joy. The evening walks and the night sails. The bending down on the floor beside her, haunches in the air. Songs that were shared, harmonies. She asked him what he thought of the Scottish Colourists. Had he studied the sculpture of those Meredith people who did the war monuments? She talked about poetry and this was a surprise to us because we did not know that about her, not at all. We believed her. In this transformation, we believed her, Mrs Wilson believed her, Eustace above all saw it as something real and true and what he had been waiting for all along.

One day that July we decided to pay a visit to Mrs Cowan in her chambre de bonne, months after the funeral. Freda rode the rocking-horse and her thick legs stuck out to the side and we wheeled along the far bank of the river until we reached the door and the narrow staircase and we laced the rocking-horse reins over the railings and left him waiting while we walked up those stairs like we were indeed a unit, like we shared a conspiracy of excitement. Mrs Cowan no longer looked like grief, when she opened the door, she had exchanged black for floral. Without the responsibility of her countess she was younger.

'Come in,' she said, 'come in.' She had a Scottish Borders burr.

'My, you've all changed,' she said, 'you look well,' she explained.

Tin soldiers, we stood in a row before her while she sat in Julieta's old chair and this could have been a danger moment, because there she was in Julieta's chair and there was not Julieta and in the shared memories around us was the shame – but there was no danger moment, Sybilla was a delight, even more so when Lady Grace appeared from out of the bedroom just as though nothing had ever happened, just as though the banishment of living things had been a falsehood.

Gentleman's Relish and tea out of proper cups. Something was laid to rest that afternoon. We believed that. Gentleman's Relish on Scottish oatcakes and not much was said, not many words, Mrs Cowan was more of a doer at heart, but it was as though we had all raised our cap and batted something out of guilt and into memory or we had all put our lips together and blown.

The rocking-horse stood patiently at the end of his reins and from the poplar across the street, the wood pigeon watched them, the quartet or was it the quintet, and they no longer had the look of pilgrims.

CHAPTER V

Jennifer, Jemima, the girl came almost every day. Almost every day, after school, every day. When the holidays began, she stayed all day and often for nights in a row. Weeks blurred into months and that summer was long and it was short, it was rich and it was rich again while the emotion subsided and the joy arose, while the razor blades turned into bars of soap that eased us all along, through the river of our life. All of us – all three of us, Eustace, me, Freda – welcomed Sybilla into our world as though she had been missing, as though until that point she had not been there at all but just a phantom, just a promise. Sybilla danced from fifteen to sixteen on a cloud. She learnt poems and declaimed them on the deck in the evenings when we were ploughing, when we were harrowing and tilling, when the farmer's year was going from longest days to shortest. She came home with the girl and they would tip their bags out onto the table where we ate and there would be books, three or four, four or five, Stevie Smith and Sylvia Plath, Jean Rhys, Enid Bagnold. I write this sitting in the kitchen sink and they sat there in the sink and while *The Rite of Spring* and its pied cavalcade incarnation flowed from the mind of the clock master through my fingers via a frenzied cats' cradle of thread into a growing, monochromatic pile in our cabin, Sybilla did indeed transform – from distant to present, from brooding to giving, from concave to convex and I mean that not in a physical sense but in the sense that now she leant into life, not away from it. Looking through his drawings again, which I never saw Eustace put to paper, I see again that everything about her from the colour of her eyes to the way she held her head to her poise, they did transform – more than you would expect in any ordinary growing child – and it was only later that I understood that this transformation was mirrored and equalled in the artist and above all in the artist's work.

For that was the moment when the bestiary, his strange, wonderful idea of commemorating the unsainted past of our grandfathers, grew up. From the child-sized models he had moulded in clay along the edge of the table when Sybilla was just seven or maybe eight; from the nights when he dreamt it, when I knew he dreamt it because there was a restless stirring quality to his sleep; from the talks he gave – that one he had given when Julieta came for tea and stayed for his performance with spoons on the boat and he talked of the use of the beast form,

'I choose the beast form to represent this army, Julieta, because in those wars, men had become beasts; the generals were bestial and the men were bovine slaves. And yet this will not be to undermine the cow or the horse for they are finer than man and all the sacrifices they make are unknowing, blind unthinking generosity to their masters. I see the bestiary as something that connects us long into the past, an extension of cave painting where the cows and the man shared the same rocky canvas, an extension of stone monoliths and giant circles and mountainside chalk engravings. We may think, Julieta, that we are not animals either inside or outside and I say and I believe that we are both. We are cows and we are horses, we peer over the cliff to intimidate, to protect, to defend and we peer over the cliff to frighten ourselves with the future, to look forwards, to imagine and inhabit the ghosts we will become, to make ourselves feel all the four corners of our souls, for we are afraid, we are great, we are nothing.'

Looking back now, I see that they were hopelessly intertwined, the father and the daughter, his happiness becoming increasingly contingent on hers. And I see that this became more so, the more she grew, the more courage she grew, the more her friendship with the girl held up a mirror to her, showed her what she could be and how the world could be in her presence. The more of-this-world Sybilla seemed to be, the more Eustace came to depend on that fact, his bestiary, his goliath project growing wings at last, from beyond the mind and the talking and the maquettes and into a real thing, like the opposite of playing spoons because first he was conceiving the music and then he was giving us its conduit, the spoons themselves.

PART IX

THE GIRL

CHAPTER I

Over time, I came to think of her as one of those cardboard figures from a Victorian paper theatre. This was wrong in many ways because she needed no manipulation, no prod. It was also wrong because she was far from one-dimensional. But I thought of her as having appeared in our lives as if from above and staying in our lives held from above and she could have danced in or out and there was nothing that held us to her but the fact that Ann of Goole embraced the space where we all happened to be. If life is an oboe, if an oboe is only there to find the hole that holds the air that vibrates to make the music, Ann was our oboe. The girl, Jennifer or Jemima, she became one of its vibrations.

She dressed in lace, in patterned fabrics, Liberty, swirls of red squirrel browns and malachite greens. Lace at the sleeves and lace at the collars and I asked her one day if she made her own clothes because it seemed she must and she smiled, we had something in common. One pair of shoes, she had found them in a junk shop she said, they looked like the ones Charles the First wore to the scaffold, black, petite, blocky heels. One coat that trailed the ground, frogs and fur, deep blue, wool, must have belonged to a soldier. Everything about her body was on show, everything was for sale, blunt, shameless – and then the contradiction of the collars and the lace and after, when I came to speak to her once Sybilla was finally found, I tried to read this, to see through the layers of her and decipher whether she was a true extrovert, whether her frills and furbelows were it, were her, whether it was a richer and more complex story than the one I wanted to believe.

Sexy and smart. She was definitely those things and as time went by and she became more entrenched in our lives, she grew more into herself. Yes, she still stole food hot from the pan and yes, she made me doubt myself as the mistress of Ann of Goole, as the woman who inhabited the space I stood upon. And yes we grew used to her, nearly fond.

But there was always that side to her, that adrenaline of her, that danger of her. Gold-plated self-confidence in one so young. Catch-me-if-you-can insolence. One day I found her sitting at my sewing machine because I had been outside with Freda watering the tree peony on the roof of the main cabin and into one of the black-and-white costumes which was sitting unfinished on the table she had stitched the word WHORE. I came in as she was standing up. I looked at the word. I looked at her. She looked back at me. She stood up and walked off.

The girl and Sybilla wrote poetry together, automatic writing they said, and beneath the layers of truly wonderful invention, of strange juxtaposition and dreamy albeit teenage language, I felt a sense of mockery, of my, our being mocked, of the world that

Eustace and I had so carefully constructed having been infiltrated by someone who did not always mean us well.

They drew together, automatic drawing they said – and now I find these sketchpads hidden under her cabin bed, now that Sybilla has gone – and I see that Eustace was a feature of these, caricatured, sometimes kindly and humorously depicted and sometimes I have to put the pad down and gasp because they were not kind, not always, they were wrong. They drew him – and I think it was they – as a cloud and he passed over their faces, over the faces of the girls who sit on the deck of a boat that looks like a galleon, and light is blocked out. It could be shadows from sails but Ann has no sails, she is a barge, a heavyweight carriage horse whose power comes from behind. In some of these drawings, the ones I put in a pile named Drawings to be Burnt on the Fire and Thrown out to Sea, the shadow has distinct human form, hair and hands. Emphasis in many of the drawings is laid on the hands, hands that are grooved and pitted with work, with lines of dirt, hands that are moving, shaping. There is one sketch where the shadow sits next to a girl and he is poised over a table along the edge of which queue small indistinguishable figures. I am not sure on which pile to put this drawing, Drawings I Should Send Back to The Girl in a Cardboard Box or Drawings I Should Use to Paper Over the Cracks in our Lives. The lines between cruelty and humour, between memory and imagination are blurred, in this work. I sense the power of the young from them. I sense the fear the young can wield over the old. Out of the mouths of innocents.

When I look at these drawings as I am looking at them now, I know that the girl knew this, that she understood the power of the young over the older. She knew that that sense of freedom to act as you please, that lack of fear of authority was a weapon. She could confound us, menace us, menace the people in charge, the structures in place and if she had no fear herself of anything at all, there was no sanction. Look at me, she could say, you can't catch me. Look at me, I am light-footed, I am smart, you are at my mercy.

It is strange to be judged from within. It is strange to feel that a bird has descended into your nest and only when it is too late do you understand that the bird is a cuckoo.

CHAPTER II

Sybilla began to stay at the girl's house. It was my fault. No, it was Eustace's fault. No, it was our fault. She asked if she might and Eustace said of course my angel, of course. He believed in her transformation – it was a gold-leaf, hand painted, hand carved, one-in-a-million icon for him, a point on the map of Nowhere that showed him where to go and how to be – and now Eustace could not afford to lose this because whatever it was, it had become so precious. He worshipped this icon, this point on the map of Nowhere. He worshipped this transformation. Of course Sybilla should do what she wanted. She should take her transformation and share it.

One day I went to the girl's house to collect Sybilla because I had news, wonderful news and I wanted to talk to her about it, *The Rite of Spring*, the tours that were coming, the big film studio, the more work that would come in my direction. I wanted to tell Sybilla this news because I knew that when my grandmother told me things like that, up on the north shore, with the clipped hedges and the long, long light, those were the things I remembered, those intimations, those secrets.

I wanted to tell Sybilla this news because with my

mother, it had not been like that, she had not shared with me, not her news, not her feelings. My mother's was the guidance of the Delphic. She sat in the same chair, with the same posture, she deliberated over papers and bills, she worked on projects that I never knew about or understood. I can see her now, in profile, head tilting forward on her neck, glasses on a string, long legs poking out into long shoes. Between us there was love but it was shrouded in hierarchy and old rules and, now that I think about it, in fear – not my fear of her nor hers of me but fear of it, fear of that love. Still I am haunted by the one time when I made her cry, by the one time when I did something that forced her out from beneath her time-old carapace. It was not meant, I had not meant to, I had just passed on something whose weight I had entirely not understood, something my grandmother had said, some comment, about my father I remember, about her choices. Old tears, tears coming from a body that did not cry, that did not show its feelings. The thought that I had done this when I was just a girl, repeated something by rote, wounded my mother, inadvertent, artless, thoughtless, that became my fear, that I might do it again, that I might break something I had come to regard as unbreakable.

And her fear? Well maybe it too was tied up in that moment. Perhaps it was that she did feel, deeply, so deeply that she dared not show it, so deeply that if she did show it, it might burst out and be too much and she would lose her grace and she would lose a bit of herself. That moment, if no other, had shown to her how delicate the balance was that she struck, defending those choices, remaining the elegant, long-legged, long-shoed model of composure, protecting herself. All this she strove to hide, and but for that one time, she succeeded so well that the last time I saw her, when she was dying from the inside out, was the first time she told me that she loved me.

Of course I loved my mother because you must love your mother, you must and she gave me music and she left me all her papers and the clavichord and I saw that she had had a life, indeed she had, just not one that she shared with me. But we did not have a conspiracy. We did not. She gave me music because she loved it herself, because *Casta Diva* or the *Four Last Songs* or *Quartet from the End of Time* would rain from her soundbox on Sunday mornings and I could not help but absorb that. She gave me music and it was wide-ranging, surprisingly catholic in its spread and I suppose if I had understood that then, I would have seen her as an altogether more complex, open, sentient being than I did when she was alive. Likewise with all the other things she gave me, I did not recognise them until it was too late, she had left.

Regret. Sorrow. I had sat with her for just five minutes. It was just before I left for the city. It was a long time before I had bumped into Eustace on all those separate occasions. My father had long since gone. He had taken his thin knees and his strange addiction to chopping wood and moved on. I sat with her in a cell and the profile I knew so well from her sitting in the chair was stretched out on a dais of the dying. I love you, she said, I love you.

I wanted something different with Sybilla and Freda. I wanted to make different mistakes, not the same ones. I wanted to have a conspiracy with them, I wanted them to know me, weaknesses and all, more than as a mother. I wanted them to look through my papers after I had died and say, ah yes, I remember that, ah yes. I wanted them not to be surprised when I said on my deathbed that I loved them. I wanted them to have known all along that this was the case and to have heard me saying so enough times that any deathbed repetition I love you would be a comfort, the resumption of a chorus that they knew and loved themselves. I wanted to make that for Sybilla and for Freda, to make it that I did not just tell them what to do but that I showed them my vulnerabilities and asked them to help and I shared with them my excitements so they knew more of me than just my role. So that day when I heard the news, the designer of the pageant of *The Rite of Spring* news, I gave it no thought, I rushed round to the girl's house and it was the first time I had been there.

CHAPTER III

About the girl, about Jennifer, Jemima, we knew very little. Don't ask me, she said with her wide eyes and her thick hair. None of your business, she said. She was like that, cocky, distant at the same time. I knew nothing about the house she lived in or the family she lived with. I had an address and I marched there, almost jogged there, my heart bubbling, it was not far from the basin, and it was a small cottage in a terraced street with a door red as the colour of kings. I knocked and a man answered and he was old, at least in appearance, and there seemed to be nobody else until I saw plumes of giggling feathering down the stairs.

'Name's Albert,' he said, 'I'm her granddad. Hardly see her these days,' he said.

I had the strangest feeling that this house was twenty times larger than it appeared, that twenty times more stories lurked within its walls. Where were the girl's parents? Seemed like there were none? I looked at the sprigged wallpaper with pictures of castles and at Albert who had combed his hair from one side to the other to cover the baldness. Everything was neat.

Everything was ship-shape. Spick and span. And yet there was a looseness, an infinity, a kind of anarchy that I could not either see or hear or smell but I could sense. I sensed it like you might hear it in the opening to the *Eroica*. It was some kind of emotional cacophony that I sensed, some kind.

'Sybilla! Please will you come. Please. I have something to tell you. Something exciting.'

Albert stood there with his hair over in thin links over his white shining skin. Spick and span and spick and the giggling stopped and I wanted to go up there and I wanted to bring her down the stairs with my excitement, with my come-with-me, listen-to-me, because she was fifteen, sixteen, she was floating on a cloud of transformation and I too did not want to lose her, not now.

'Sybilla! Please will you come. Please.'

She did not answer. I know that she heard because the giggling stopped, the plumes evaporated. There was silence. There was nothing. Silence tumbled down the stairs like the red stain that would come over the stage and seep into the stalls. Nothing tumbled down the stairs. I saw the nothing and it was wrapped up in twenty times of stories. I looked at Albert and he fiddled with his false teeth, in and out, over his lower lip. He shrugged.

I ran. I do not know why but I ran from Albert's house, away from the silence, away from Sybilla who had stopped giggling and that was all. All at once, the feeling I had had when Sybilla was a baby and we were helpless in the chambre de bonne with the days never-ending – it swept over me. I was just here to let her be here. I was the oboe, the space that defined where she was and now she had no need of me. I had no power, none at all. What use was my love for her if she did not want it?

Before I saw him, Eustace saw me. He saw my face. He was in the wheelhouse preparing for a night sail, I walked towards the boat from the east and I thought he would run out and up and over and he would lift me up and put me down and he would go to the door that was the red of the colour of kings and he would knock and he would sweep Albert off his feet with all that bluster and then bring her down so she could hear our news, so we did not have to fear that she was leaving us. I thought he would sense when he stood at the bottom of the stairs with the granddad flicking his teeth that the girl was somehow not good for Sybilla, even though she had been a wonder, a transformative wonder. I thought he would feel the pull of all those stories and know that unhappiness lurked there, that the girl – sexy, smart, scallop-thieving – was made from unhappy things, that we should call in our Sybilla card, shout out Queen of Hearts, shout out Royal Flush, shout out Snap! or Jinx! or Spit! and make them turn their heads away so we could be sure she came with us, so we could be sure.

I tried to tell him. I tried to say that I was afraid we might lose her, transformation or no transformation. I tried to say that when he went to the house with the king-red door he should not let it show, he should not roar like the lion he was, he should use his gifts in the ways God had granted him, he should keep his paws soft and his tread soft and he should not show how vulnerable he was to her, to the fact that there was a gap between them, that he nursed a wound and it was in the shape of her, in the shape of the mistiming and the misunderstanding that just would keep arising between them.

I do not know what happened. He left the wheelhouse. I could hear the boom-boom of his tread from here to there, from Ann to the terrace. His tread was not soft and that was not good. I could hear another boom, running alongside, the rattle of his heart, the pounding of his blood. Freda was wearing a pair of dungarees that I had made from the offcuts of *The Rite of Spring* costumes. She was black and white, linear, Vasarelyesque. She was still puppy-fat pudgy and the lines bent and waved with her contours and if you looked at her for too long, it made you swoon. Freda had a passion for the flowers, for the watering and planting, for the putting into pots, for seeds and tomatoes and the tree peonies and bulbs. For the camomile which we had planted into a rooftop lawn. We climbed onto the roof and began to tend them, she seemed to understand them, she could put her fingers in and tease out last year's growth and know when they were hungry or thirsty. She was only seven or eight but her feel for the world of the plant was that of a seasoned grower. Piggy-shaped squeals emerged from her black-and-whiteness as she found the hint of a new shoot or the germination of a seed. So there we were, on the roof of Ann, Freda in her very own Elysian Field, I waiting.

I saw him come back at last. How long had he

been? I did not know whether he had taken a year or a day or no time at all. He was alone. He would not say. He would not say what had happened, he would not say. The coaly black sack of nothing was there again, bulging. If he had a plug in his heel and it was slightly adrift, I would not have been surprised. Ichor had left him. There were spots of it in his wake.

CHAPTER IV

How had it come about so all-of-a-suddenly? A few days later, the girl came round and asked if she could pack up a suitcase and take Sybilla's things back to her house? It turned out that a suitcase was already packed, had probably been packed for months, she knew exactly where it was, she must have known all along, she was lying when she asked to pack up a suitcase, what she was asking was to collect the suitcase they had packed together. I asked her if I could come and see Sybilla up those stairs behind the red door and she said sure. If she wants you. I asked her to explain if anything was wrong, if Sybilla had herself explained what was wrong, if we had made mistakes, what were they, if we could put things right, how. It was too much. I should not have asked her that. She was smart and cocky but she was not an adult, adults had largely been absent in her own life, I saw that when I went there the first time and sensed the stories.

Eustace was at the workshop when she came, putting the final touches to the horse I shouldn't wonder, he had borrowed a comb of mine he said to make the mane sing, he had borrowed some lengths of thread so he could make sure the whiskers appeared to blow. I asked too much and Jemima or Jennifer she looked at me as though I was mad, an imbecile, a child of the workhouse. She did not answer. Freda had soil on her dungarees and I stared at the brown patch that was spoiling the monochrome and thought I must wash them, I must make sure I love her, Freda, enough, I must not show my fear to this girl standing before me with the pre-packed suitcase, with her wide eyes and her thick hair and all the power.

CHAPTER V

In the post, a letter. We did not recognise the handwriting but we knew. We knew it was from her, we knew. I was there when the letter arrived and I knew and I put it on the ledge on the port side beneath the porthole and it stared at me all day, while I waited for Freda to finish her day at school, while I waited for Eustace to come back from the workshop where he was spending far more hours than he had strength for.

I was about to start on the costumes for the chorus of young girls. It was time, all the others were done. For a cast of hundreds, this meant weeks, months more work. One single costume would be different from the rest. One would not be part of the black and white, part of the dizzying optical illusion envisaged by the designer. One would be the singled-out, the sacrificial. I had to ponder how that would be, to make it logical and yet unforeseen. The designer had said she thought that I could find it, it would rise out of the work I did over these coming months, it would reveal itself, this one costume while I worked on all the others. Freda came back from school and she wanted to visit her nasturtiums and the letter stared at me from the ledge. She picked them, a few of them, pulled the trumpets off the back, squealed when she found an earwig, squealed when they were too peppery. As she did every day, she asked me when Sybilla would be back and I could not answer but I showed her the flower heads sprouting from the dahlia corms and together we picked bugs off the honeysuckle and she wiped the fronds of the palm tree with a chammy.

There had been no night sails since the suitcase was taken and Eustace and I opened the letter later, deep draughts of wine later, when Freda was in bed asleep holding to her chest a black-eyed Susan that I had stitched for her out of dark green and amber yellow felt and a piece of the blue velvet which had been used to cover Sybilla's chair. Deep draughts of wine and we stood in the wheelhouse, sides touching, the clock watching and opened the envelope, bracing ourselves for its words.

It was not written by Sybilla but by the girl. They were going away. Albert did not mind, it said, he was fine about it in fact. It was asking for money. It was asking for quite a lot of money. It was not asking for anything else though, not for permission, not for blessings, not for forgiveness. It was not offering anything such as explanations or even calumny. To accusations and complaints, we could have responded and in doing so, felt – albeit misguidedly – that we had some kind of traction in this. To a request for permission, we could have been generous. To a demand for money...

By my side, I felt him tremble. I felt his tremble come up from the wheelhouse floor. It was deep like the tremble from the ground when plates are beginning to break apart. It moved upwards, through his legs, through his belly, his chest and into his heart and I could hear something that was not voiced but it was tears, the tears of a giant of a man who sees he may have lost the thing he can least afford to lose. Or maybe it was tearing, the sound of rending, the sound of a heart imitating paper, ripping. All those members of his family whom he lost before, if not in fact then in memory. The mother who left him, the father who left him, that stuck-together duo of selfish thoughtless humanity who imagined that it was their dreams that mattered. That stuck-together duo who brought Eustace into the world and could not see that in him, they could realise far more dreams than they could in a touring bus or on board a pleasure cruiser or down the wormhole of self-indulgent self-expression that they called art, their art. The aunts who did not leave him but were not with him, did not seem to recognise him as a human person, viewed him as an impediment to their own ongoing sourness. Do I sound angry? Yes, I am angry. Jennifer or Jemima or whatever her wretched name was had written a letter that in the name of all rudeness was vicious. Perhaps the rudeness was not intended. Perhaps Sybilla had not known its contents. Perhaps Albert with his combed over pate had dictated it. I doubted all of those things.

We made love – beneath the sheet and the blanket, with the dawn breaking over us – and his tremble went through me still and I was damp with big hot drops of his pain and wracked with the premonitions I had felt all those years before, when she was born.

PART X

THE MONEY I

CHAPTER I

Now it was my turn to be afraid, to be haunted by afraid. Not only about Sybilla but about Eustace. His tremble was a stifled roar, grief and rage and grief and the sudden return of all the memories. I saw that Ann of Goole and the steps he had taken to be where we were, in her, working on her, together most of the time – these were his gestures towards protecting himself from the abandonment, the bitter early lesson he learnt about selfish stupid people. I saw that his love for Sybilla, his need for her love was not just that but it was a shield he could wave about in the battle against the idiots, in the battle to remind himself that his family, his parents and aunts, had been useless. It was not only that he loved her dearly and he felt that they mistimed their shared love; it was that he could not afford not to be loved by her, that his were the fingers clinging to the cliff-edge, his was the sensibility made from the most delicate material. His love for Sybilla was his love for himself, she a small girl-shaped mirror that showed him the truth of himself, that reminded him he was not just a man but sentient, that he was not just mortal but this side of mortal, alive.

There were no more night sails, there was no more flashing of pans, there were no more roars of pleasure at the small things, the minutiae, the nearly eating an earwig, the almost falling into the water, the news announced in a letter from Mrs Cowan that Lady Grace had been to the vet and pronounced not a lady but in fact a lord.

I was working on the chorus girls and something came into my sewing that I had not known before. It was as though fear gave me freedom, as though I was losing my vibrato, giving way to the song in its purest form, as though the blindness of panic was a ticket. The chorus girls slowly rose from the table and each was imbued with something I had never managed to impart before. Is fear love? Is fear a handmaiden to love? Is fear what we need to sew well, make well, dance with more jeopardy?

We had to decide about the money. It was not simple. It was not. I read the letter over and over again and determined not to give any. I decided I would sew the letter. I took each word, the sum, the currency sign and all the zeros and I stitched them into the garment where the word WHORE had been stitched earlier by the girl. I did not think she was a whore but I did not think that the zeros deserved to left alone, they needed to be tormented, re-ordered, sewn in red, made unforgotten. I stitched them upside down and the wrong way round, the words, a zero, money, another zero only this time shaped like a banana, the sign of sterling pointing at you as you looked at it, the central spar sharpened into the blade of a directed knife. I made it comical and I mocked it. I made it sinister and it mocked us. I hoped that by sewing it, I could gain dominion over it, that we could wrest back something from the horrible shock of Sybilla having left and Sybilla having been party to a form of blackmail. We would not pay, we would not pay, it was blackmail and that word too I spelt in anagram form across the cloth.

Eustace walked in while the black and whites were being peppered by oversized, flat-on-their-back zeroes and I saw him, his face, his clinging to the cliff-edge and I knew what kind of blackmail it was, that we had no choice, that if I loved him, I had to save him, that if I loved him, I had to save her and that if I loved her – and of course this was not just his heartbreak but it belonged to all of us – they had both to be saved. And I knew that we had to pay the money because there was no choice, no real choice, not then.

CHAPTER II

I dreamt of zeros and whitening fingertips and
a shining pate of spick and spanness. I dreamt of
trembling and I woke with the tremble running
through me and it was not mine, it was his. We have to
pay the money. He sat next to me and his hair bowed
down. He sat next to me and his hands, lined with
clay residue, with tiny bits scraped from the moulding
of the horse, perhaps the outline of its whiskers, they
folded together in a here-is-the-church, here-is-the-
steeple origami of pain. Do you know where they are
going? Can we ask them that at least? Can we talk to
her, before she goes, before we give the money? Can
we bring her here one time and sit her in the chair of
her choice, your one the green, mine the red, and show
her? Show her what she is to us? Show her that she
is too young for this? Show her that this is what you
had and it was not your choice perhaps but it was not
good? Remind her. One more night sail. One more ride
on the rocking-horse or at least one more journey with
the rocking-horse, perhaps Freda up? Can we walk her
along the river on the other side, beneath the gaze of
the wood-pigeon and undo the mistake we made about

Julieta, walk up the narrow high-ceilinged staircase, wind up the pianola, bring out the spoons and you can make them dance as you did before, that time when Julieta came to the party we held on Ann of Goole? Can we buy her a cat? A Lady Grace or should I say a Lord Grace? Can we write poems for her, ones like the ones she has discovered with the girl? Can we make her automatic drawings into a collage and paint them across the sky from heaven to heaven, from cloud to cloud, from one end of this sainted city to another and paint above it a heading that says Sybilla Coldwinter, WE LOVE YOU? Can we go again in the old car with the gramophone blaring out her favourite, maybe *Wandering Star*, down the bumpy track, down to the far end of the river where we walked along the coastal path like sheep? Can we make Hat-Man again? Can we find the suit I made for him that she put somewhere and fill the suit, with all of our imaginings, with all the words we remember she shared with Hat-Man, with all the journeys he made alongside us, can we try, can we try to bring him back? Can we do anything, Eustace? Anything at all?

We both went to the girl's house and we drew Freda behind us on the rocking horse and this was not a ruse, just a practical necessity. An upstairs window was open when we reached the king-red door and Freda heard the giggles of her sister, they were circling out over the street and our younger daughter dismounted from her steed like a true stunt cowboy, fat calfs bouncing as she leapt to the pavement and she banged on the door before we could, shouted out Sybilla, 'billa, brushed past Albert whose teeth must have still been in a glass somewhere, Sybilla, 'billa!

Please come and talk to us, Sybilla. And the noise upstairs was joyous, so joyous, sisters exclaiming as one, that afterwards I wondered if Sybilla was doing what she was doing out of choice, perhaps the girl was forcing her, blackmailing Sybilla in turn. Sybilla came down the stairs because she had to, because Freda had pulled her. She looked at me and I could not read her look. I wanted to throw myself at her but I knew that would not work, she was trapped inside herself, inside her own complications and this was made worse by her age, by the swinging of her pendulum from red to green and back, by her once concave, now convex, now concaveness. Eustace bounded forwards. He inadvertently knocked Albert against the panelled wall of the downstairs, against the wallpaper sprigged with castles. It was a tiny thing but suddenly it spiralled into a fight, Albert saying Oi, then Ow, the girl sticking her head out from her bedroom, over the banister and barking down the stairs that we should leave, screaming that we should leave, we had no right, Freda crying, darling baby piggy Freda suddenly exposed to something miles from earwigs and tree peonies, Sybilla – had she been about to let us in – suddenly withdrawing back into her trappedness.

The king-red door closed in our faces and we turned left and we walked away. Eustace carried Freda and she buried herself into his shoulder. The rocking-horse wheeled along and if rocking-horses can be sad, if horses can tune in to the feelings of their masters, of their surroundings, then he was sad, trundling-with-moan along the street, bumping into lamp-posts, into the raised edges of the paving-stones, truculent with sadness, bow-backed.

CHAPTER III

We had to grow accustomed to the quietness, the emptiness on the boat. Shockwaves piled on top of her absence and we sat there in our own chairs like fools. We wrote letters and sent them to the little house. We tried to push out of our minds the memory of taking a bag full of pound notes and handing them in shame at the bottom of the wallpapered stairs to the girl. We tried to push out of our minds the thought that we were getting this all wrong, that we should handle this in another better way. What other better way was there? We tried to resist, we did resist the temptation to go to Mrs Wilson and ask for her help because we were afraid of what that might unleash, the words that might pour from the girl or indeed from Sybilla, in front of Mrs Wilson who already disapproved of how we were, I just knew. I wished that Julieta could bring us some of her old grande dame wisdom but that was ridiculous, she was dead. The only thing we could take consolation from was the fact that they had not gone anywhere after all, they were still in the house with Albert, still going to school, it was the last throes of the academic year.

Eustace wrote her a letter to invite her once again to visit where he worked, this time I have something to show, he said it out loud, clear, in proper written words, his hand-writing pared back as though he was afraid in his enthusiasm he would push his pen through the paper. I have something to show you Sybilla, please will you come to the workshop, bring Jemima, bring Albert, bring all your friends, I do not mind, I would be proud, I love you. A note came back saying when? and Eustace was over-the-moon joyous, let's go for a night sail, he said, let's have spaghetti a la vongole, let's throw parsley and garlic and three sheets to the wind. She is coming, he said, she will come and we stood in the wheelhouse, the three of us, Freda on his shoulders, and watched the clock watch us and watched the river allow us to cut through her. Houses and lives and gardens and small parks and walking dogs nodded and dipped as we wove past, shadows followed us and speckled us from above, the sun dipping down while larger-than-lifeness blew us forwards. She is coming. She answered when?

He had forgotten. Not just the weeks' interval but the content and form of those weeks, not just the silence but its heaviness. The little house that held her haunted us, man with false teeth, bald head bobbing in and out of visions, thousands of stories, anarchy of stories. The picture of all those pound notes being held, for what exactly, for what. The times when I said to him I thought the money was not demanded for its usefulness but for the power that it gave over us. We had ceded. We were dominated. Surely that was it, the girls – our daughter and the girl – were still there, they had not left. Whatever plan it was they had, it was still to be evoked. Eustace buried himself in the horse and he said the whiskers were as soft as silk, he said the mane, you could stroke it. I worked through the chorus girls, slow, slow like I had anchors tied to me. They were better yes than costumes I had made before, they seemed to hold bodies before the bodies entered them, they spoke of the pageant of womanhood as though they were the pillars in the Alhambra, every one slightly different, every one a blind.

When? she had written and Eustace replied now, today, tomorrow, as soon as you can. This time he did put his pen through the paper and his reply disappeared into another week or two of silence, after we had got back from the night sail, the speckles of the shadows now freckles, caressed by the grin of the moon-and-stars clock. Now, today, tomorrow and after a week or perhaps two, an answer came and it said later, after I come back. The party he had planned, the meat on sticks and the wine in goblets and the three cheers from all of them at the workshop, the flares and the flags and the faranfara – they all had to be put away. Later, she said, after I come back. The horse remained in his stable or at least on his plinth in the corner, its mane soft enough for you to stroke. There was no pendulum on the moon-and-stars clock and the grin never altered and the long eye-lashes always twinkled. We could have borrowed a pendulum as a metaphor for the party that Eustace had planned and his excitement, for the swing as a letter arrived and the swung as its contents were absorbed. We could have wished that the smile and the twinkle could tune in to us and alter but time was the only thing then, in that toing and froing between us, that was certain.

At last we heard that the girls had gone, left the little house, moved out of town. Eustace went and spoke to Albert and he tried not to push him against the wall when the old man told him he knew nothing, honest, hardly see her these days. Sixteen now, what can I do? He shrugged and Eustace told me he was minded to buy the old man a new set of false teeth that would not jump about on his lips.

CHAPTER IV

Before she was found, I came to persuade myself that what we had done was to pay Sybilla to leave. We had agreed to their demand. We had given them the money they asked for, each penny of it. Was it a test and we should have said no, you may not have this money? Was it a test and we failed it? Were we tacitly sanctioning what they did? We did not mind that they wanted to leave, in fact we were glad, we paid them to go. I wondered if that was how the girl would have seen it, that she and Sybilla would sit up late into the night with their automatic writing and automatically write or draw our failure. 'See, I told you.' Now it was not a big cloud overshadowing Sybilla and her friend, it was a big wind blowing them away. Would they draw us as the wind? I had to be careful, I knew the girl was not bad, they were young, she had been brought up surrounded by stories that were hauntings, that were bad acts by bad people. I had to be careful, I could not bear to think that Sybilla was with someone who was bad. I had to hold on to the fact that they were fragile and we were dealing with fragile things and there was no right or better way, only the way we could see.

A letter arrived. From somewhere on the south coast. They were on the south coast, a letter arrived, Eustace, she is ok, she has written! The postman had arrived early, we were up early every day, waiting. I snatched it from his hand. We felt old when we opened it, sitting next to one another, hunching over a single small sheet of lined Basildon Bond. Now as I sit here I can remember the smell as I tore it open, the noise of the double lining of the envelope as my finger tore through it. We felt old as we sat over it, old as we leaned our heads against each other's, old as tears sprang to our eyes, she was not dead, she was not on another continent, she had not forgotten us.

They were working at a cherry orchard. Or a fruit place. Or a vegetable farm. It was all of those things, drilling, sowing, weeding, lopping, threshing, harvesting. Blackbirds, she wrote, nest outside the barn where we all sleep and I wondered what 'we all' were like, were they safe, were they brave, would they see off the fire-breathing monsters that in my dreams were circling round her? The word commune wafted through both paragraphs, they were working together, pulling together, there was a man and he told them everything, what to do, what to pick, how. Do not come and find me, she wrote, but we did not mind that sentence, it was the others we cherished, old, hunched, tear-wet cheeks.

We bought a map. I ran from the jetty to the street to the old newsagent where the shopkeeper wore a brown shop-coat with brown shop-coat buttons, mid-calf length, no darts and I bought a map of the south coast and I ran back, my hands feverish, my heart, my too big shoes. It was still early and we unfolded the map on the floor where Eustace had bent down with Sybilla all those times and shaking fingers found the place or at least near the place or at least probably near the place. Fat pudgy feet propelled Freda, tousled sleepy Freda, up the stairs and she looked at us both bent double like Hunca Munca and Tom Thumb and rubbed her black-eyed Susan against her cheek. Sybilla?

By the other end of the day, Eustace had mounted the map on some board and I had found one of his old easels with a dragon detail on the top of the stand and the map took centre-stage, pins in it, pen-marks on it, a big red balloon with the name Sybilla written in big black letters across it dancing from a promontory at the bottom where we thought she maybe was, maybe.

CHAPTER V

A kind of ease settled over Ann. An uneasy ease but an ease all the same. Letters between us and I let her know how Freda was getting on, ten now, eleven now, Mrs Wilson's favourite because she was excellent at netball and a demon at cricket and always cheerful, always. Freda misses you. I wrote that in every letter and it was the sentence that went unanswered, without fail. Eustace wrote religiously, daily, sometimes twice-daily, how are you my darling, I miss you my darling, you are an angel, you belong among the stars.

The letters filled the spaces between us, filled the time we might have lost. Looking back, I see the letters were probably a more honest and in-depth exchange than we had ever enjoyed with Sybilla in person. Though never at length, she wrote in raptures about the blossom and the serried rows of fruit-trees and the work. She did not refer to the girl but she did to the man in charge and there were times when a note jarred, he sounded as though he might be a bewitcher, a child-catcher, lie this way, face this way, wash now but it was not in our interests to worry about something we could not see when there were so many other things we could. She wrote about the evening light, she wrote about learning the song of the blackbird, taming the blackbird, feeding the male with raisins from her hand. She wrote about bending over, all day long, digging potatoes, first earlies, the pleasure of drinking water when she was smeared in dust and sweat, squatting down on her haunches in the furrows and spraying it from a flask over her head until the mud turned to stripes down her cheeks. She wrote about no machines, only hand labour, hand-sowing, hand-tilling, hand-threshing. She said her arms were brown and muscled and she had grown an inch, at least.

Eustace said read this and she had told him that she was happy, that she loved him too, that when she came back, they could walk from the boat to the workshop and she would put her hand over his arm and perhaps they could skip. She said I am happy here and I am sorry.

By then, Eustace was deeply involved in negotiations for the placing of the bestiary. The men-cattle were not made yet, the site had to come first, he was not entirely alone in his enthusiasm but it was a job, to find somewhere, to find town fathers, cliff fathers who would agree that yes, that this should be. Away from the workshop, he sat at a desk we shared in the wheelhouse and the moon-and-stars clock watched as ink and words were spilled in a fury of you must, I must insist, can't you see, can't you see. Problems were spun at him, no time, what about the weather, dangerous, too big, too bold, too surprising, money, precedent. Problems and he sat at his desk and used his old Parker with a medium-sized nib as a bat and he squared up to the problems, lists and lists of them, and knocked them into the boundaries one by one.

Eustace had been dreaming of this project for the past ten years, or maybe more, perhaps since the day he was left on his own at the gates with the fuchsia detail. All this time scaling it out of his imagination and into his notebooks, into the mini statues he had lined up along the table's edge. In the meantime his work had been monumental yet largely personal, gravestones and tombstones and once a set of pyramids for an Egyptian businessman who longed for Luxor. Mostly they were objects of the day to day or at least they were well within his scope or at least they had become within his scope by now and he longed for the challenge of the bestiary, for not only its technical difficulty but also its artistic complexity. Completed, it would become one of the biggest of its kind. Completed, should he find the spot, it would be seen not just from land, from the sea-shore, from the river but it would also be seen from the sea, out at sea.

In some ways, I realised, we were engaged in a similar challenge – the pageant of men. Showing them as a phalanx, showing them as individuals. Lambs to the slaughter, cows to the slaughter, a cow to the slaughter. Sacrifice – and this was chance, we were unconnected in our work – bound our daytime efforts, me at the sewing table, Eustace at the desk of infuriation.

Days flew by in a blur. With Sybilla's avowals of contentment, we were able to pursue our work. I was stitching time, I saw later. The bodies that would fill the costumes I was sewing at my table were growing from young women to women and I was making this, deciding this with every seam and every tuck. The moment would come for fittings and then time would regain control and the hours of *The Rite of Spring* would be lived in, like the bodices themselves. Night sails intervened, one in particular, October, the month of cider-making, and for once we went against the river and into the city, as far as we could, given the depth of Ann's hull. Freda took the wheel and shrieked when she saw the landmarks, the huge tower, the huge clock, the folding bridge. Eustace for a while stood on the roof of the cabin and his giant shadow played on the water, a spectacle for those ambling along the banks, daydreaming. Darkness fell quickly and we were guided as we turned by the cats' eyes of street-lamps and lights in office windows which danced on the water in front and behind, above. The lights were orange. The lights were white and silver. Strings of them waltzed like fireflies and Eustace, Freda, I, we were entranced, standing in the wheelhouse, a trinity.

Somewhere on the south coast in a barn, Sybilla was lying dust-ridden, exhausted, hands dry, happy, waiting in her sleep for the song of the blackbird to wake her.

PART XI

THE MONEY II

CHAPTER I

A few days after their night sail into the city, there is a storm. It is an out-of-the-blue storm. It is not predicted, not precedented. The skies turn. They were the blue of an Indian summer and now they are yellowy, dirty grey. Winds are born. There are no squirrels. There are no birds in the air. Leaves on the street gather together and dirt and twigs. All at once – and it is early evening – the winds grow and they smell of menace, the winds are menace and they circle, down then up and around, down to the water, up to the masts, around the bodies of the boats. Rain joins the winds, not wet rain but dagger rain, not wet rain but soaking rain, soaking, drowning rain.

The oak tree watches these winds and begins to give and take from bottom to top, from root to bough, bough to root. The oak tree watches the grebes as their feathers ruffle from behind, as they are swept off course on the water. The oak tree watches, beginning to wave and bend, to whip back and forth more and more fiercely. The oak tree watches and the oak tree feels, as the storm grows stronger, stronger. Dusk comes and goes and the night closes in and the winds grow angry, enraged in their blindness. They speak, spluttering, words indistinct but the meaning clear as though this were not murky night but bright brilliant day. Why are they angry? The oak tree has never seen them so. Some ropes snap. A mast blows over. A boat detaches from its mooring. Water – normally still and untroubled – grows foamy and aggressive. The oak tree can hear the water. It can hear the gods within moan and grumble for they have been asleep for many years and do not like to be disturbed. The oak tree can hear the clouds and they too grumble, every time they are lashed against a building or thrown against a mast. The oak tree feels the rain. It drives needles through its leaves, it drives its leaves to depart, stinging, stung.

The storm lasts for a night and much of the day following. In colour, it moves through sulphur-yellow to black, through brown to red, burning embers tinged with black, a force of nature that is alight, breathing fire, creating havoc. In sound, it is dissonance. In words, it is blank verse, free verse and yet this storm has its own grammar, it must have. The oak tree, exhausted after almost thirty-six hours of trying to stand still, trying to hold its gracious posture, allows itself to rest at last, leaning a little further over the water than it has done for the past two hundred years. It closes its eyes, weary, worn out – and this mournful sight is echoed across the basin. The Phoenix lists dangerously to starboard. The Pride of Antwerp has lost its rigging to the water. The Mermaid of Bournemouth is wedged half in half out of the water, beached.

And just in front of the tired old tree, Ann of Goole, semi-submerged, the Dolphin having plunged a knife into her side.

Alongside Ann, in the grimy dirty waters, a rocking-horse and a small suit and tens of black and white costumes and papers, like nothing means anything any longer.

CHAPTER II

The papers! The drawings of the bestiary and all the details and all the negotiations and all the lists with all the problems! My costumes! The chorus girls and the black and white and the white especially and all the care! The tree peonies, the pots, the nasturtiums that are nearly over now, the garden, the gardens, the roof-top, the camomile lawn, everything! The water, it is still coming in, Eustace, Eustace, I love you, where's Freda, sorry what, sorry what, the wind, Eustace, the rocking-horse, its stable, shall I tie them, can you help me, it's too heavy, crash, what's that crash, look at the Dolphin, coming towards us, unmanned, Eustace, we need help, Eustace, the oak tree is leaning, it is falling, Eustace, I have Freda, she is in my arms, I have Freda. Eustace, the map, the map! Her letters!

CHAPTER III

In all the years, they say, in all the years in all the memories in all the volumes of the diaries of the sailors and the boat-people who have lived on this river for all the years, there was no storm, there has been no storm like the one that leaves us, after that night and day, with our lives soaked and smudged and torn and stained and splattered. The Dolphin dislodged from its mooring, old ropes, decayed ropes, and on a current of sudden unforeseen ferocity, motiveless, made a direct line for Ann. The Dolphin is not wooden but steel and has acted like a razor blade, scything into Ann's side until she moans. The damage is not enough to sink Ann because Ann is a Boadicea, a behemoth, a former Humber barge used to the vicissitudes of open waters, but it is enough – with the winds and the rain from above – to leave her leaning, to propel the stable and the rocking-horse overboard, to wash half of *The Rite of Spring* costumes and most of Eustace's bestiary papers into the basin, to sweep away the roof-top garden so lovingly tended and nursed by Freda, to mock us, to make us feel stupid and small and ill-prepared for this life or indeed any other.

We stand on the quayside, clear of the drooping oak, and watch Ann as she gathers herself, creaks and gasps and sighs and long low groans of exhaustion. We are worried she might die, such are the sighs of pain, so long and plaintive. You could almost say she is writhing. You could almost feel her agony. We stand and watch and we stand and weep and even Freda is lost for smiles because the scene is truly horrible. Everyone is standing. Everyone is lost, in this moment, overwhelmed with loss. We are all soaked. We are all exhausted. Someone from a boat further down the quay leans over into the water and pulls out a pram. It is empty of course and we all feel empty, we all do.

Gradually the winds land on the ground and die and the clouds and the rain blow away and the sky clears, as though to mock everyone there who has lost 'most everything. The coots emerge, they were hiding in the recesses of the basin wall and already they are arguing. Men are moving towards the Dolphin on a tug, leaning into the Dolphin, ropes around her, chains, screech as she dismounts from between Ann's ribs, towing her back to her mooring, new ropes. Water is still. Leaves are still. Velvet and sequins and the tail of the rocking-horse and the small suit, the one I made for Hat-Man and have never seen again until now. Floating, not moving far, not far at all. The map, detached from its board, leaning limply against the jetty. And her letters, confetti across the basin, symbols of love we thought, proof of love but the paper was cheap, no more Basildon Bond, and they drank in the water and drowned.

In the bright morning, we stand. Pieces of white, ruffled feathers, splintered wood, shattered wood, steel pierced like flesh. There is a smell. The smell is fungal. There is a tune playing and it would sound good at the death of an unnamed street-dweller. People gather to watch. To look at the ropes and listen to the shouts and in some few cases to wade in and swim in and gather up. And all we can do is stand. And we stand and we stand and we stand.

CHAPTER IV

So now everything has changed, or that is how I feel, how we both feel, how we all feel, faced with the capsized prospects of our passions. There are three kinds of future and they are all spooling around us, the quick-gather-up-the-papers future and the how-will-we-survive-this-future and the please-may-I-lie-down-and-sleep-forever future.

We cannot stay on the boat, it is not safe. We cannot. We cannot stay at the workshop, it is not safe either in a different way, blades and things, furnaces. Mrs Cowan! Perhaps we could join her in the chambre de bonne, just while we sort out the futures, just while we go to bed and lie there and sleep forever.

And we limp along the river with anything that is not sodden, that we might need, that we are afraid to lose sight of. There is a new blur and we are in it. The winds mock us with their absence. The skies mock us with their calm. Ann of Goole, behind us, is still, on an angle, a half-beached matriarch, pride shot.

The wood pigeon sees us from atop the poplar and we are once again like pilgrims. We are trooping under the tree, we are crossing the road, we are pushing open the door, no horse to tie up, we are going up the stairs to Mrs Cowan's door. She says of course, you poor things, you poor poor things, she is in her florals, a bit of lipstick now, a sharp bob, the little space painted, anti-macassared, decked out. The sink is no longer stained and the high window is clean and the door closes behind us as a blanket might come down upon a bed. It is as though the storm never took place, there are no branches down here, no papers scattered. Lord Grace wraps himself around Freda's ankles and in the little kitchen the red kettle whistles. Eustace says you stay here, Isabella, with Freda, and I will go back and I will see to Ann because there is no time, very little. I want him to stay. I want him to lie down in bed with me forever and Freda beds down next to me and it is like I am back in the Georgian house with no name, lying on the floor and reconnecting to a time when everything was yet to happen and there was no money.

Because yes, the storm that no one predicted has brought not just a work disaster but a financial one. The costumes, the time, the damage, the papers. Eustace leaves us at once before I can object, before Freda can throw her arms round his belly, jumper loose with water, hair lank with undried rain, through the blanket-closing door, down the high narrow stairs. He leaves and behind him words like workmen, words like welders, words like salvage and mortgage and commission and fortune, will cost a fortune linger in his wake.

Mrs Cowan – Hilda – is marvellous, wonderful. She agrees to take Freda to school each day and fetch her back each evening while I trot to the basin and go to salvage what I can, to help Eustace as I can, to work on mending Ann before she disappears into the dark depths where the water gods have barely ceased their grumbling. There is a tug boat and a crane. There are huge straps and hawsers and everything we know and love by now is sopping wet and woven in and out of rubbish from the jetty, rubbish from the water, flotsam, feathers, blown-away-other-people's-stuff. The crane groans as it heaves Ann sopping from the water and hangs her, out to dry. Men come. They stand around. They point at the hole. They point at the point of the damage, its extent. They point at other things and I stand to the side, like a hopeless female person because I do not understand about welding and hulls and I do not wish to hear the words, all I want to know is when, when can we mend her, how soon, when will she be mended and we can move back on board and we can go back to how it was, I can go back to my sewing and Eustace can go back to his bestiary and Freda can make again her garden and maybe soon, one day soon, Sybilla will come home again.

Eustace turns to me. They have handed him a piece of paper with some numbers on it. I open the piece of paper and I nearly collapse right there, to the side of all the men, it is more than we have, more than we could ever have, how can it be so, how can it be so?

CHAPTER V

The basin descends into silence. Even if men are shouting, even if boats are being levered out of the water, even if broken masts are being pulled about and hauled about, even if tears are being shed as precious things – letters or bestiary notes or the face of the moon-and-stars clock – are being found and they are dreadfully damaged, in most cases beyond-the-pale damaged, the basin is silent. I cannot find my balance. I cannot put everything back into the right order, Sybilla, Freda, *The Rite of Spring*, Ann of Goole, Eustace, the bestiary. Should I write a letter or should I mend a hole or should I stitch a new black and white bodice to replace the one that was irreparably stained by a week in dirty water? Should I dive into the basin and sweep through and pull up all the left-over mangled tatters of our hold on Sybilla and see if they can be made to mean something still? Should I hold myself round the waist and stay in the chambre de bonne and smile, every time Freda walks close, smile with the resolute cheerfulness of the idiot? Should I cry? Should I weep for what we have lost? Should I go to the place where I think she is and tell her what has happened and ask her if she will come and help us, if she will come and put us all back together?

I do not think it is the same for Eustace. The list of things he needed to retrieve is as long but he has not lost his balance or at least it does not show. Perhaps he is made for this, for having too many things to mend, I do not know, I hardly see him at nights and in the day he has his head down bullfighting his way back into the life he fought so hard to contrive. Eustace, my darling, shall I go and find her? And then he does pause, it must have been on his mind every moment, he begins in the middle of a sentence, should go there, should carry her back, should share this with her, she would come, come. I am wrong, he has not lost his balance, he is almost losing his mind. Inside himself and he is a stramash, bolt-cutters and trying to dry out her letters and remake the map and the bestiary, the cavalcade of lost ghosts and of course, her, the statue of her that will be mounted on the perfect-maned charger that awaits her.

Bills come in. A knock at the gate from the metal man, another from the tools man, another from the chandler. Word comes from the studio that plans for the bestiary are moving forward, he needs to come and talk to them, he needs to work on it now, do it now, where is he, how can they keep him on if he is not there, perhaps they should do the bestiary themselves, take it back in hand, yes it is his project but now where is he, where? Word comes from the ballet designer, where are the chorus girls, why so slow, why so silent, why?

Frenzied. Panicked. I make him sit down. We need a plan. I make him look me in the eye. We need a plan. I list all the things. The boat is still holed, still hanging from the crane, wounded. Freda is with Hilda Cowan. I list all the things and we try to see our way forwards and then another letter comes and it is from her. We are sitting down, trying to list it all and the letter appears and I think it bears the same postmark as the last one and it says more money, it is asking for money, why have you not written, why? Four weeks and we have been circling in an eddy bequeathed us by the storm. Eight weeks maybe. December is coming, the days are short, how can he weld in the dark in the rain with the frost biting his fingers? He has left things, we both have. Left the work and the bills and the things that need to be done. We need a plan. The words – more money – and I want to stitch them into the cloth with the word whore and burn it, burn it with my eyes and my rage, burn it with my tears because fuck that storm and fuck that girl. He is so broken. I have never seen Eustace so.

We go to bed. I drag him back to the chambre de bonne and we slide onto the mattress in the room we are using. Freda is at one side. She snuffles. Wriggles. I undress him. His arms are heavy. He lies down in the middle and I climb in after him, it is the first time he has slept for weeks, and I hold him from behind and the tremor of him ripples the sheets.

*

He welds and beats. He bends and twists. I hand him rivets, I hold up plates of metal, I sluice and shovel and paint and sweep and right. He sweats and bleeds, he grinds and bashes. I mop and dab and soothe and whisper and hold out cups of water or pieces of ham.

Words have left him. All he is now is a weapon of determination, a one-way ticket to I will survive this, we will survive this. Grunts, groans, bellows perhaps. I repaint the face on the moon-and-stars clock. I hang up Hat-Man's suit on a fence. I dry out and wipe and dust down the rocking-horse, plump up the stuffing of the saddle, burnish the bronze studs, wax the reins with fat until they grow soft again. Winter makes it harder, days short and as it happens bitterly cold this time. The eyelashes on the moon-and-stars clock grow frost even though they are inside the wheelhouse because not all the windows have been replaced yet, not yet. He grows pale and thin from the endeavour, from the all-night, all-day labour and one day he says he is doing all this now, all this in this way so that we can go and find her, sail the river, find the place on the coast even though the map is gone, even though we have lost most of her letters, even though Albert is a half-witted imbecile, take Ann of Goole and land there, sweep her up, back to where she belongs, where she belongs.

I will not let it happen he says that I leave her. I will not.

*

But he has to return to the studio because that is where the money is made and he has to regrasp the bestiary as his own because in his absence it has grown away from him. Others have understood the power of his idea and they are mooting sites and schemes and renditions that are just shy of his concept but in any case it is not their project, it is his, driven by his vision, his past, his making hands. The bestiary sprang to life while he was sitting with Sybilla on deck and she tipped her head to one side on the table he had made out of yew and he was damned, damned if someone else was going to take it from him. No sooner have we got Ann back into the basin and moved back from the chambre de bonne and feebly re-hung the velvet sequin drapes that were still good enough than Eustace has to go round there, to the triumphal arch-high brick wharf building and beg them, charm them, smile them, laugh them, hug them, show them, talk them, that this is his, that he must be allowed to resume it, that no other man can make it as he will. And then he has to do what he promised and make it happen, make the spot be chosen and the cliff burghers agree and develop his vision of the bovine slaves so that you know, as a passer-by, you know exactly the story they are telling.

I will not let it happen he says that I leave her. I will not.

PART XII

SHE IS LOST

CHAPTER I

Tout se casse, tout se passe, tout se remplace. Those are the words of a wise woman swathed in swan's silk and ermine stoles who is watching us from her green tomb and shaking her head, in sorrow or admonishment I am not sure. The debts mount but the boat heals, the tremor goes into abeyance and it might be late December or early January or almost Easter, it might be beyond remembering since Eustace last played the spoons or we ate Gentleman's Relish or the four of us slithered down the ribbon of the river on a night sail.

Still we cannot send the money, because as yet there is no money, because we have had to pay the metal man and pay the tool man and for the hiring of the crane which they insisted was cash up front. We have to pay some rent to Mrs Cowan for the space for the mattress on the bedroom floor because we have to.

But we write. We write it all. The storm. The boat. The hole. The work. We miss out the bit about the map and the letters and we do not allow ourselves to imagine that she may no longer be at the address we last had. Albert says when I pass him in the street that he has heard they are in trouble and I ask him how he has heard and he shrugs, he says just heard. After that we write every day. Or Eustace writes. Or I do. Sometimes just a line. Sometimes pages. Darling we miss you. Darling the boat is nearly mended. Darling we have hardly any money, we will send some as soon as we can. Darling please will you let us know that you are well, that you are safe, where are you, how are you, Freda sends you squeezes, we love you. The rocking-horse is dry now and better though some of his dapples are not as bright and the brass studs are not the same. Hat-Man's coat is in your room, on your bed, waiting for you and so is Freda, she has planted you seeds, she wants you to have flowers when you come back, seeds that she shook out of pods from the plants around the basin and they are all colours, Sybilla, yellow for your hair and blue/green for your eyes and pink for your cheeks says Freda because she loves you darling, she misses you, we all do.

Eustace writes about his work. The cow-men and the men-horses. The animal-women and here and there an animal-child. Do you remember how we made them out of blobs that day? Do you remember how we made that telescope for Julieta that day, so she could look back into her past and remember the knights at the balls and the men in their primrose-yellow tailcoats? Do you remember that you promised you will come and see my workshop, see what it is I am making for you? Do you remember the calf that was born before we left the farm, it was a fine red bull, I think I will use him as my model, what do you think?

She is lost. From the arrival of her letter in December, through January, through February, over

Easter, we hear nothing. Albert's mutterings – when we beard him or bump into him – are runic, in spite of his new teeth. In trouble he says again but it is possible he is talking rubbish, that he is losing his mind, the words clattering and splattering into nonsense on the front of his lips. Might he be more of a child than the girl he was entrusted with, we wonder, and we screw pieces of cloth in our hands into twisted knots. Do you have their address, Albert, the correct address? And he says 'course I do' and that is as far as he can go.

She is lost. We must have the wrong address, she must have moved on, perhaps she is in trouble, why did she not give us her address in the last letter, no maybe she has not moved on, if she wanted money, she would have said, where to send it to, she must be at the same place and she is not replying, she is not replying, she is lost.

CHAPTER II

She is lost. We say it as we work. As I pull back together the white and black, as I begin to replace the costumes ruined by their immersion in the basin waters, as I grope to re-find the balance and the rhythm swept away by the October storm. We say it as we write letter after letter, as we wait every day for the post and there is no reply, as we go round and bang on the king-red door and try to elicit some kind of sense or clues from the old granddad who is losing his mind, he must be. We say it when we go to bed and when we rise from bed, we say it as we nurse and cajole Ann of Goole back to health, we say it as we stumble on, scraping together money for the tool man and the metal man. I think now that we said it to ourselves not because we believed she was lost but because we could not believe it, because we thought that if we said it often enough, somehow the thought would be devalued, become meaningless, become wrong in fact.

She is lost. Sybilla is lost. She is lost to us, we will not see her again, it is our fault, we have abandoned her somehow, Eustace, you left her, Eustace, you did what you swore you would not do, Isabella, you just stood by and watched.

We discuss it. We will go and find her. We will drop all our tools and sail there, walk there, crawl there to where we think she might be – and we will find her. And yet the truth is that even if we could summon the energy and wherewithal to go down there, to find the last spot on the map that we had marked and which we might just recall if we tried, even if she were there when we sailed or we walked or we crawled on all fours to the shed with the blackbird and the us, the we-alls, we do believe she is lost. Incantations or no incantations. Double-think or no double-think. It is not that we do not believe it. It is that we do and that we are blinded and paralysed by the thought.

Through that May, through that June, through all of that summer, we tell ourselves she is lost and the hope that might be couched behind those three small words, stitched and moulded inside and around them, becomes risibly thin. We continue to send letters but we are no longer surprised when nothing comes back. Freda stops asking about her. The rocking-horse, standing in his deck side stall once again, looks more doe-eyed than before. The moon-and-stars clock is not yet ticking again and perhaps that is a metaphor for the thing, time has stopped, we are not moving forwards.

Increasingly work takes over. *The Rite of Spring* will be filmed in its field of stubble in late September. They are building a stage, for although this is film, it is theatre too and the designer is shifting between settings in order to comment on the nature of sacrifice – earthy and primeval and on a titanic scale on the one hand; cloistered and mannered and small on the other. Rehearsals begin to take place in July, when the corn grows gold, and I lose sense of myself as I pull back the chorus girls into the shape they were in before the storm, as I think through exactly what the final costume – for the nymph to be sacrificed – should look like. The designer, the clockmaker comes to visit me one day on Ann of Goole. She is tall. She has long lines down her face, all vertical. Everything about her is long, her silk skirt, her wrists, the line of her nose. Will you be ready Isabella? Will you be ready? She clicks in the back of her throat, sounds like she is choking on a small bone, will you be ready? We talk about the designs. The monochromatic heap that was lying on chairs in our cabin, then floated across the basin, is now remade in Sybilla's room. I have suspended lines of rope across the ceiling and we hang costume by costume from the ropes on coat-hangers. The size of the cabin requires that the costumes are hung closely together. There are five lines, six lines and they run parallel. From the door, you see them lined up facing you. I see the pillars of the Alhambra and a tribe of women and pagan may not be black and white but still this will move you, this scenario will move you, it will dazzle your eyes and dazzle your hearts. Here is the corps de ballet, here. Here is the final scene or the pivotal scene, here is *The Rite of Spring* as Stravinsky or Diaghilev or Roerich would have longed to imagine it, earthy yet not, blind and anonymous yet not. I look at the designer. Her name is Helma. Now I know that Sybilla is ebbing from my mind because her room has become the set and because when I look at Helma, I smile at her, at her long face and her long grooved cheeks, at the cut of her skirt which is perfect for that face of hers, perfect.

CHAPTER III

Eustace has found a spot, a perfect spot, a cliff overlooking a fishing town where the church is high, on the top of a hill in the centre of the town, its steeple reaching up towards the cliff edge. It is towards the end of the river and beyond, river on one side, sea the other, not our river but one that goes into ours near the end, by the same sea. Eustace is talking to the town burghers, reminding them of how it was just forty years before, reminding them of the waiting or was it fear or was it terror or was it defiance that their forebears felt as they sat in the path of the enemy. He is reminding them that they may not seek to revisit their ghosts but they are surrounded by them, the sea is awash with them, the rocks against which their sea crashes are full of the fossils of their fathers and grandfathers and is it not time to break them out of their chains of death and make them above ground, above water? He says – and I am listening while he addresses them all in the hall that is partly for meetings such as this and partly for the school – that this pageant will bring you eye to eye with the past, eye to eye with God and with War. Yes, Eustace says, yes. In doing this, I will meet

God and War. My beasts of War will look into the eyes of God. The sea will look upon them all. Sailors of the past, ghosts from the sea, will know that this is an act of devotion, a salute to courage, to folly, to death itself. Fishermen will see it as a new kind of beacon, no longer the cliffs that they must avoid but the shrine that they must respect and revere. They will pass under the gaze of the beasts, look up into the gaze of the beasts and they will know what they have lost, will know what has been lost, who has been lost, will understand that there is no past, only art. War and the folly of war should be fought with art, with blobs of bronze wrought by hands that sit and stand as memory, reminders of what should not be repeated. Courage and death should be enshrined in such reminders. Men should be represented as cows and animals because, as he told Julieta that time, they are no better than that and at the same time, almost as great. We are beasts, Julieta, beasts.

It is a bravura performance. I watch the audience, the mayor here, the corporation there. I watch the fisherman and the other fishermen. I watch the people who know the sea and the people who simply live there. I watch the old-timers who have never lived anywhere else. I watch the women, above all the women, because they are the ones he needs to persuade. There is one woman in particular, she sits apart. She could be Mrs Wilson with her arms folded across her chest. She could be my grandmother with her I-am-proud-and-fierce etched in her demeanour. This woman is not a woman of men, I think. If she can be swayed, it will happen, I think. I watch her watch him. I watch her listen to him. I see her like my mother and my father and all the people, not flashy, not fancy, stubborn, suspicious.

Eustace is making ground. Lips are unpursing. Crossed arms are uncrossing. Furrowed brows are ebbing smooth. I understand something about Eustace that I had not understood before – he is not simply my lover or the father of two brave, spirited bundles of daughter. He is not simply a man dogged by a childhood that is lost or by the memories of mothers and aunts who did not care a whit for him. He is not simply a sculptor who has a vision. This Eustace does not put his hand to his mouth or allow his hair to fall into his eyes. This Eustace does not allow his big trousers to slip. This Eustace would not be cowed by the petty admonishments of a second-rate headmaster. This Eustace would not be baulked or halted in his tracks by the difficulties of rendering a nude onto his paper. This Eustace is a man, a sculptor, a thinker, an orator. He is a beast himself, a being of power, lust, endeavour. He is a lion.

I do not have the exact extent of his plan for the bestiary in my mind's eye because mine is a memory that is laced with threads and lined by fabrics. Three-dimensional perhaps but not architectural. I do not see as he explains it now, the line of figures and how it/ they will change the village below and the sea below and the lives of people whose eyes stray upon it. What I do know is his passion, in his words, in his gestures, in his fixedness. There is a slight tremor in his voice, a tremor of you must see that this is good, not an orator's tremor, not something contrived and false, no, it is the tremor of conviction, of I must win them over, I must. When his monologue comes to an end, the townspeople in the little hall are indeed won over. Lips smile, arms swing. It is hard to read the face of the proud-and-fierce one but there are no open words of disagreement. A hammer meets a gavel and it is decided. I feel almost as though I do not know this man, as though he is now making a journey alone. Perhaps he must do so, in order to drive home his message to the aunt who laughed at him, to the aunts who resented him. To send a message in a bottle to his mother and father, a message in spirit and in bronze. To show his girl that she was wrong, he loved her with all his heart.

He is pleased. He pummels his thigh with the heel of his hand when he hears the news, when the gavel bangs, when a man with a tie comes and whispers into his ear that the cliff can be his. They go out to the pub, into the rain because there are winds that night, out of the rain and into the Fisherman's Arms which is bright and smells of salt and I sit down in the corner because this is his day and I watch him from my seat while he holds them. This is Eustace. This is the man I love. This is your father Sybilla, a great man and more than that someone who loves you more than life. I want to write this all for I too am in his spell. The noise rises and Eustace grows, taller and more ebullient than I have seen him before. I think is it because he has spoken? I think is it because he has managed to conquer them with this idea which he has held so long in his mind? I think is it because when he does this, makes this, realises this, he will speak again, not just through a message in a bottle but through one that will chime across the waters. Perhaps this vision for the bestiary will drain him of all the things he has forgotten. All those cells that are left inside him will go out and in doing so, he will remember them. Everything he has will go into this great monument and everything he has to get rid of – before it eats him up from inside, the loss, because the roar of him and the yawning chasm of him are overwhelming.

Why can she not be here to see him, his verve? Why can she not just come back, just be found, write, then come or not write, just come? Follow him to the workshop where he can show her the horse he has made for her, the horse she can ride for always if she chooses, forever. Let herself be swept up and picked up and roared at by this man I love, this man who loves her so deeply.

Where are you Sybilla, why don't you just come back?

Eustace and I go home to the boat. Axe-Happy Sam is there and he comes to raise a glass with his friend and Freda, sleep-heavy, watches Eustace get out his spoons and he plays like a banshee and later we almost go for a night-sail.

CHAPTER IV

I understand that I have never told the people at the theatre what I mean by lost. The word has assumed its own meaning to them for they assume that she is missing. I have never told myself what lost truly means. Eustace and I believe she is lost but nor have we discussed what we both mean by lost. We cannot mean missing because otherwise we would go to look for her, we would assume that Sybilla's missingness means that she wants to be found. Missing would mean she went against her will or by accident. It means intransitive. Missing would be something done to her. Does lost therefore mean that it is something she has done? What is she lost to? Or from? It cannot mean that she is floundering because she has never floundered, I do not remember a moment when she seemed unsure. Of course the day Hat-Man went but on that day she was not unsure, she was bereft.

Now I come to think about what it will mean when she is found, what will found mean? Will it mean that Sybilla walks back to the boat, along the jetty, knocks on the cabin door, sweeps up Freda in her big bright look, pulls her into her cabin with the

Hat-Man suit waiting for her on her bed? Giggles will rise, squealing. Will it mean that we go on all as though it has never happened, as though she has never swept out of our lives with a girl, a young girl, and asked for money, quite a lot of money? Will it mean that I have to find that piece of cloth that is embroidered with the word WHORE and all the zeros and pretend it never existed? Will it mean that we forgive her, for the bad dreams and the bad days and the bad nights when we felt too old and too ill-equipped to withstand the fact of her having left?

One day I am standing on the roof of the cabin of the boat and I see Jemima or Jennifer, I am sure it is her, at the far corner of the basin. I am sitting cross-legged on the camomile and the smell of it is warm in the sun, around my knees, spongey and warm. I stand up in a jerk, it is her, it is her, and I knock a red geranium and almost kick it into the water and although it does not fall, a shower of its petals does, red tears streaming down the side of the cabin and onto the water. I climb down and I run down the steps and along the, I don't know, the razor blade of everything, the razor blade of hope because maybe Sybilla has come back, maybe she is found, maybe she has come back. If lost means that she does not want to be found, found means that she wants to be found, that she chooses to return. Found means I should run like the wind to the place where the girl is standing and throw my arms around Sybilla because she will be there, next to her. Found means that I should stand somewhere high and wrap my hands around my mouth and shout out to Eustace, wherever he is along the river, EUSTACE!, she is found. Found means that I should burst into Mrs Wilson's class and try not to frighten Freda while I pull her by anything I can get hold of until I can explain and she can run with me and she can run with me.

I reach the place where the girl was and the girl is not there and Sybilla is not there and Albert is not there and there is no one in the vicinity who seems to be able to help me. No one has seen a girl whatever her name might be, Jennifer, Jemima, Sybilla, it makes no difference, either they are blind or I am blind. What does lost mean? I sit down on the spot where I thought she might be and I know I said this is not my story but the story of Eustace whom I love and his daughter whom we both worship, but today this is my story. It is spooling around me in tears made of red petals. It is spooling around me in debts and words written in love that are drowned. Every night I go to bed and through a prism of rehearsals, of black and white, of tortured zeros, I feel myself being revisited by that feeling that swept over me when we were hurtling into the room where she was born. We have not sent her more money. We have not received letters from her since shortly after the storm when she asked for more. We are at her mercy. I am at her mercy. I am sitting on the ground in a pool of red petals that are tears. There is no smell of camomile and there are no velvet sequinned curtains overhead and I am sitting here. Where are you, Sybilla? Why do you not answer us? When will you return to us? Please tell me, Sybilla, which one of us is lost?

*

That night when he comes back and all I want to do is change everything, everything we did, everything we did not do. I want everything to change but him and Freda. I look at him and he has burst into the role of chef, omelette for you Madame, fines herbes, champignons, oui? Omelette for you, mademoiselle, avec fromage, oui, des tomates? He has wrapped himself in an apron that I made for him a hundred thousand years ago when I was going through a chestnut phase and he looks like a brown bear. Freda watches him while he moves the pan around as though he were conducting, sing for me, Kathleen, sing for me, Edith, an oratorio of bears, of brownness. I ask him where he is with the beasts, how he is going with them, the last time he told me he was modelling the part-man, part-bull which was not a minotaur, he said, it was a man with cloven feet, red-haired pasterns, red the colour of that bull-calf. I ask him how many, do you know how many, because sometimes he thinks there should be thousands but he knows there cannot be, too much bronze, and he says no, I do not know how many, not yet my darling. Bread? he asks and I say I thought I saw her today, the girl, I thought I saw her and I ran as fast as I could but she had gone or she was not there and nobody could help me... and Eustace puts the pan down and he turns to face me and the violins and the cellos and the oboes and the horns and the singing and the music stop.

CHAPTER V

The rehearsals. Helma stands in a pulpit looking Druidic. Black and white chorus girls float through the stubble field, meandering through the score by the great Russian whose story is both ancient and eternal. One of the dancers has slipped, it is the dress rehearsal and although we are only in a notional stubble field, not the real one as yet, the costume has torn. I am looking at a rip and through it at a leg that is shuddering with effort.

Yesterday or was it last week I showed Helma the costume I have made for the girl of sacrifice. It is as it had to be, it is as it must be, Helma's long face saying as much and her words. All the women. I think of that as I put the finishing touches to the black and whites, to them all. I think of it as I look down back through the corridor of mothers, my own, hers, Eustace's – whom I never met. I wonder why the teacher let him go to the bench alone in the dark and did not check that Mrs Coldwinter was waiting. I wonder at myself. I turn the spotlight on myself. What kind of woman am I? What kind of mother? I stitch up the tear in the dress above the trembling thigh and think that all I am is someone who makes things. I make them and I set them free. I make them and I hope that they are good and better, a twist on the possible. I sew a costume for a sacrificial girl and I invest it with something I sense, with a drop of the hard-to-grasp, the out-of-reach, the instinct that haunts sleep and not logic. Where were my instincts for Sybilla? Or was she the hard-to-grasp, the out-of-reach and it was I who made her so?

September is here. The time has come to go into the real stubble field. It is time to make the film of *The Rite of Spring* for real now, for real. We go – the cast, the orchestra, the designers and dressmakers and all the people – in coaches and charabancs, in chariots and chaises to the field that belongs to the farmer who owned the cow that bred the fire-red calf. We build a camp. Hundreds of small white tents climbing up the slope, looking out over the little shed-house where we lived once, over the sea beyond that. Sun scythes in as it did when Sybilla sat in a papoose on his back and we stacked bales and laid hedges. Sun scythes in and catches the burnished gold of the barley that has been missed by the threshing, catches the red of the poppies that nod from the margins. A stage has been built that is the size of a forest. Pipers are there. Timpanists are there. Dragonflies glint. Swallows line up on the fence that divides us from the sea and you might think they were perching there to watch. I am standing by with threads and needles. My fingers are tired now because of all of this. And yet they are not because that is my pleasure, my joy, my absorption to wrap people I have never met into costumes that will define them, to define the people first perhaps and sew those imaginings, to mine the space inside me where my hands and my eye and my dreams can meet. I am carpenter and I am doctor, I hew and I feel.

The window for the gold of the stubble is short and though the sun blesses us, we have little time. By the penultimate day, they are filming the final pagan ritual – black and white chorus girls turning like the tigers while the single chosen one remains invisible. How many are in the cast? Maybe a thousand. Maybe a thousand black and white costumed girls moving over the stage that is the size of a forest. Over and over, round and round, a dizzying kaleidoscope of diagonal, vertical, horizontal lines wave in one direction and sweep in the other against the dying embers of the gold. The stage is not visible, beneath all those feet, but it is finally covered in red, viscous red, poured from buckets unseen. The red finds the edges and the centre and it pools forward. Viscous, it moves slowly. You do not see it at first, it moves so slowly, and then the sun catches the fat edge as it rolls inexorably into the camera's view. The climax moves towards the camera, the black and white dancing reaching some kind of penumbral frenzy, the ooze coming and coming. This is death and this is art and this is life and this is dreams. Suddenly, in the midst of the dancers, one girl removes her costume. Of course beneath she is red. She is all red. There are no buttons and no joins visible and she is swathed in an all-over garment that comes to cover her face as well as every part of her. It is the red of the geranium petals. It is the red of tears that float on water and do not want to sink. It is the red of sexy, the red of thick dark hair. Red, all red and the girl falls down onto the stage and the ooze goes round her and the ooze goes over her and it bleeds into the foreground, seeping off the stage and into the earth where all red fluid must go. The scene is slow. The scene is relentless. The scene lives on that evening and the following, after the cameras have stopped, after the acting has stopped because something happened in this field, something that was half way between God and War and life, something that said everything, both finite and infinite. In the small white tents that face the sea, a thousand girls remove their costumes, in silence.

CHAPTER VI

Eustace's bestiary was made and Eustace's bestiary was unveiled and when he went back to the little hall that was sometimes used by the school, as they prepared to hang out the bunting and wave high the flags, he explained his vision further. War and the ghosts of war, men and the ghosts of men, women and the burning pride of life. Eustace stood up to leave the hall and the people of the little fishing town had been swept away, further into the rip tide of his imaginings and they cheered, the gavel rang out. Eustace – the sculptor, the visionary, the lion – was carried on shoulders up the hill and onto the cliff where the beasts lined up. The proud-and-fierce came along as well, cautious at the back but she came. The bunting was hung, the flags were waved high. There was light from the flares that lined the path up to the cliff and along the cliff, as the sun dipped. In a crocodile we trooped up, Eustace the head and shoulders. Up there and when they put Eustace down, he stood and the wind was blowing – as it always did – up from the sea. At first we all stood. Rasp of the blow in the flames of the flares. His beasts had their backs to us, their faces to the sea, their bodies, some of them, leaning forwards into the passion that had made them. We stood and we looked up. We let our eyes rove over the giantness. Eustace stood too, humbled I believe by his own creation, humbled because it had become – in the doing – something greater than he had imagined. Out to sea, a fog-horn blew and it sounded like Gone Away, it sounded like the last lament. Fog came in and now the flames of the flares were made of wool. We were muffled, we were cushioned one from another. We began to move among them, all of us, all the fishermen, all the mayor and corporation, the man with the tie, the publican. The beasts were mythic in scale. We could walk between them. We could put our hand round the thigh of a bovine slave or the leg of a woman with cloven feet and lean over, look down upon the steeple of the church, upon the sea beyond waiting to claim more memories, through the long telescope of the history of war and God and stupid selfish people who see nothing. For an age, it was silence. For an age, we were caught in a dance.

Eustace stood that night with the wind on him and all the people murmuring at last and then promises of a night to remember in the pub, later when they scrambled back down the hill and the flares began to die one by one. As I walked towards him to join him, to be enfolded in him, to lean on him, to wait for him to whisper in my ear his dreams, I wondered whether this triumph felt good enough, whether it changed anything for him, whether the doing had been good enough or was it the finishing? I wondered if he had laid his own ghosts or simply parked them here at the end of the river he loved. Was it right that he fixed them in bronze? Had he done so in order to forget?

Had he purged himself of the guilt I knew stalked him every day, the guilt that he himself had not been good enough, that they must have left him out of disappointment in him, out of thwarted hope? Had he done this for her? Had he been saying, with this great series of monoliths, I am here, I will never leave you, this is my stake, here is my soil?

After the darkness is complete, the fog eating the last of the flares and all of the moon, after gallons of bitter ale, after the shadows of the creatures have gone from the steeple, Eustace takes a seat in the centre of the pub. It is a crinoline chair like the one my grandmother sat in when she was making socks and I see bits of his shirt pressing out between the spindles. He is not triumphant but he is. In his hands, a pair of spoons. The publican found them in his drawer at the back. Rat-tail, silver, dessert. The rhythm is slow at the beginning and he pats his thigh and he clicks his tongue. Eustace's eyes are closed and his head is pointing down. He begins to lose himself in the rhythm to sway, to tap his foot and soon you cannot see the spoons, you cannot count the clicks, you can only feel it, the clicking and tapping and clinking and spinning. It chimes in with the sound of the fog-horn from out at sea and his head is down so you cannot see his face, go on, go on Eustace and we are all in his spell.

*

Eustace moves from one triumph to another, stealthily but still magnificent. I see him as the river, flowing through the great edifices of his own imagination. Of all his achievements during his apprenticeship, during our time all together, during his lifetime, the bestiary is undoubtedly the most best. When he can, Eustace goes there and works on it more. Sometimes he takes us on a night sail – without our knowing, we sleep – down to the little town and he slopes up the hill. Only the moon-and-stars clock watches his face as he guides us there. Only in the morning do we know, Axe-Happy Sam tips us the wink.

CHAPTER VII

It is the girl who tells me. It is Jennifer/Jemima, it is sexy black-haired granddaughter of Albert, boat-invading, home-invading, life-invading, scallop-thieving, suitcase-packing, cash-demanding, whore-stitching, mind-bending, soul-bending, one-time sixteen year-old packet of chanciness and want who comes and finds me and tells me that Sybilla has been found. She bursts into the costume room of the theatre where I now work, where I am patching a tear in the fabric that encloses the thigh of a woman who is playing a man, it is Elektra, it is Orpheus, it is myth, it is legend, men as women, women as men, women as gods, furies, avenging angels, and Jennifer/Jemima marches up to me while I am on my knees, pins littering my teeth, shreds of leather sliding through my fingers.

Today it is the dress rehearsal. Today I am as far away as I have been for many months, many years from the absence of Sybilla, from the hole that enshrouds our lives. Today Helma is marching up and down, this is art Isabella, this is war Isabella, this is us, this is now, this must be, it must be great, it must take them not just to then but to now, not just to now but through now, into the future, out of the other side and into wondering, into seeing yet not understanding, into the space that we can make when we are good and we are better and we do not hold back either in the vision or in the detail. Every stitch Isabella, every seam. I am listening to Helma and I am not. My ankles are seizing up inside my boots but this is nothing, a mere nothing. I am holding onto the shreds of the fabric that enclose the thigh and I am thinking about that, only that. Freda is at school. Eustace is at the studio. I am on my knees and I am hearing Helma, I am, I am doing the best, not just the best, the most best, playing my part in the plan to make everyone who sees this production feel tears, fierce tears of surprise spring out of them like they have been stung, like until then they had not known, until then they had not.

Her pair of pointed shoes comes up close to me, clatters the floor, breaks into my hearing not hearing. At first I do not notice or at least I do not act, I carry on with this most best thing, to make the man woman, to make the woman goddess or god or avenging angel. Words might come down from the body that lives in the shoes but they are obscured from me by my absorption with this plan, by Helma and her speech, by the layers of fabric above the thigh that drape over my hair. Pointed shoes might stamp and they do and it is only after a minute, no an hour, no a lifetime that I look up at her, past her feet, past the draping layers of costume and I am frowning a bit, blinking a bit, staring into the light and at first I do not see who it is because there are pins in my teeth, because I am thinking about into the future and the space that we can make if we are good.

It is her. You! It is Jennifer/Jemima. You! I cannot speak. She leans into me, down into my face. Her hot breath, her hot spite. Her finger waves at me, points at me and each jab comes with a word, and each word joins into a sentence and that sentence brings me back, out of the into the future and right into the hole that is always there, always.

'I know where she is,' she says. 'I know where Sybilla is, she says. I know where she has been all along.'

I have no words. I am kneeling, wordless. My ankles are cramping and now this is not a mere nothing because I cannot stand up quickly enough, because I am blinded by the light and stunned, because I had forgotten for months, months and months, to worry, to give Sybilla too much thought, to keep myself permanently split in two. I unfix my fingers from the leather. I unclasp the thigh. I spit out the pins. I clamber up from beneath the man, the woman, the fury. I tremble. No words.

'It was your fault,' she says, 'it was your fault. She made me do it, made me.'

What does she mean it was our fault? I have no idea what she means. It was our fault. Now I am standing. I am taller than Jennifer/Jemima, the girl, because my red boots have heels and her shoes are flat and I can see the top of her head, I can see where a small section of her thick black hair has formed into a knot and I stare at this knot, thinking how I would help her to untangle it if she were my daughter. The jabbing finger keeps talking to me, heckling my fuzziness, heckling me right slap bang into the middle of now.

It was your fault.

What does she mean?

As though we had not tried to hold her back. It was our fault?

As though we had not given her all the money that we had at the time. It was our fault? As though we could have done better, as though we could have loved her more, as though we could have understood her better, as though we could have cared more deeply about Hat-Man, as though we did not make space for Hat-Man everywhere, in the car, in the wheelhouse, at the wheel, as though we had been afraid of her, of her fragile, eggshell self, as though we did not make her a rocking-horse and a special chair and all those dresses, as though Eustace could have been something else, somebody else, less booming, less crowding, smaller.

It was your fault, she was your fault, she will never forgive you, never.

Then she says – and all I can see is the carmine cochineal blood-red of her lipstick and her lips and the shape of her wanting, chancy mouth – my granddad says you've been asking. He says you keep going round, asking him, where Sybilla is...

My granddad says he is not feeling so clever these days, he hates it you coming round and asking, fed up of it.

So I've come.

To tell you.

To tell you where she is.

Sybilla is where she has always been.

The letters you wrote, she burnt them on the bonfire by the barn on the farm with the cherry orchard. They are ashes.

She is in the barn where she has always been.

She will never leave.

She will never come back.

She will never come back. She will never come back. Never.

In the costume room, silence. Helma, silence. My legs crumple. Down into my boots.

Suddenly I am here. I am up again. I climb up through my boots. I run. The words I take are these: She is found. Sybilla is found.

I am sitting on the bench by the cannon that no longer sings above the river that flows to the sea like a silken blue and brown and green ribbon remembering the day when I told him she was found, the moment. The voice that brings me this news breaks a silence that has lasted for a little over five years. In those five years, we have paid the debts forced upon us by the storm. We have worked the theatre and we have worked the workshop and we have spun and woven and shaped and we have written the letters that came to our minds and we have worked the silence. Freda has grown from a piglet to a girl to a young woman to a gardener to a home-lover to a boat-tender. Lord Grace has made way for Lady Julieta, a fine heir who winds her tail around our legs, when we go to see Hilda Cowan and eat Gentleman's Relish on Scottish oatcakes while the pianola pumps out *Oh My Darling Clementine* and we look back. The farmers' years pass and so too do the celandines we love, they come and go.

She has been found, my darling, she has been found. He stands up straight, unbows his back, lays down his saw and I go towards him and we hold one another as we had done in the Georgian house with the falling-down banister and the whitey-green cupola. We hold each other and we hold each other and we look back through the wheelhouse, past the rusting features of the moon-and-stars clock, through the dipping fronds of the velvet and we just know, without more words, without my retelling him what and how I was told, that found means lost. She is there where she has always been and she has chosen not us. It is our fault.

'They have found her.'
They have found her.
Sybilla is found.

We can stop waiting.
They can stop looking.
She is lost.

We lost her.
We lost Sybilla.
You did not leave her. You did not.

I sit here and wait for darkness. Eustace is with me. We wave to Freda who is standing in the wheelhouse with the moon-and-stars clock and it is ticking. We lean back, on the bench by the river. We lean back and listen as it spools along, over the foreshore, between the wharf buildings, under the bridges. Twenty river miles towards the south east, a small church steeple is peppered with shadows across its slanted self. Shadows of the cow-men and the cow-women. Of the faces of the bovine slaves. Shadow now too of a 17 hands high Irish Draught beast of nobility and war, hind legs trembling under its own weight, warhorse, war weapon, in the centre, tall and beautiful, its silver tail, its silver mane good enough to brush. Somehow Eustace has layered into the saddle a shadow of a girl, a warrior. Not a stout bronze figure but her hologram. Her presence cannot be seen by everyone. The hologram is willful and comes and goes, with the dusk, with the birdsong, with the wind. A lone woman, proud-and-fierce, looks up. The woman whose name I do not know sees the addition. She has watched him. She has noticed him at nights. She has seen a man complete a herculean effort with winches and trailers and love, with magic, with bloody-mindedness, with love. Eustace and the woman do not speak but she watches him and the stars watch them both and she is the one who can see our girl and she will know.

When the warrior shows, the girl warrior, when the hologram becomes real, becomes visible, when the horse rears and its girl sits tall and she belongs among the stars, the river moans. The river cries out. The river cries out for love.

Acknowledgements

A big and heartfelt thank you to Lynn Michell
for helping bring this novel to light.

And to my children Jake and Clara Pople
for being all round generally marvellous.